He Was It

"Ianelli—Mike?" She stopped in front of him and dropped her bag so she could offer him a hand.

Black eyes whisked down to meet hers...eyes that once and for all explained why the nuns drilled every good Catholic girl to keep a penny between her knees when she kissed. He was it. Sin. Temptation. All those good things that made up guilt.

"You're...Flannery?" His mouth curved in the beginnings of a lazy, relaxed smile.

Both despair and laughter settled in Maggie's stomach. She'd seen that smile before...the kind of smile that a man usually reserved for his favorite niece. Well, underneath the surface, Maggie had had it with that brand of luck. She wasn't interested in auditioning for the sainthood. Not this time.

Dear Reader,

Welcome to Silhouette! Our goal is to give you hours of unbeatable reading pleasure, and we hope you'll enjoy each month's six new Silhouette Desires. These sensual, provocative love stories are both believable and compelling—sometimes they're poignant, sometimes humorous, but always enjoyable.

Indulge yourself. Experience all the passion and excitement of falling in love along with our heroine as she meets the irresistible man of her dreams and together they overcome all obstacles in the path to a happy ending.

If this is your first Desire, I hope it'll be the first of many. If you're already a Silhouette Desire reader, thanks for your support! Look for some of your favorite authors in the coming months: Stephanie James, Diana Palmer, Dixie Browning, Ann Major and Doreen Owens Malek, to name just a few.

Happy reading!

Isabel Swift
Senior Editor

JENNIFER GREENE
Madam's Room

Silhouette Desire

Published by Silhouette Books New York

America's Publisher of Contemporary Romance

SILHOUETTE BOOKS
300 East 42nd St., New York, N.Y. 10017

Copyright © 1987 by Jennifer Greene

ISBN: 0-373-05326-6

First Silhouette Books printing January 1987

America's Publisher of Contemporary Romance

Printed in the U.S.A.

Books by Jennifer Greene

Silhouette Desire

Body and Soul #263
Foolish Pleasure #293
Madam's Room #326

JENNIFER GREENE

lives near Lake Michigan. Born in Grosse Pointe, she moved to a farm when she married her husband fifteen years ago. Jennifer feels that love needs both laughter and tribulations to grow. She's won the Romantic Times Award for Sensuality and the RWA Silver Medallion, and also writes under the name of Jeanne Grant.

One

Three seconds after Maggie stepped off the plane, she discovered that the Indianapolis Airport was no place to buck a crowd, particularly on a Friday night and especially if one were carrying a sleeping bag, bulky alpaca jacket, purse, and a bulging duffel bag that seemed to weigh three tons.

She managed, in time, to locate the Ground Transportation sign. Dropping her gear, she pushed back a strand of auburn hair and started searching the crowd. Since even in heeled boots, the crown of her head still only topped off at five feet four inches, visibility was marginal. Dozens of bodies bobbed and darted around her. It would have helped if she had some idea what Michael Ianelli looked like.

Restlessly, she bit her lower lip. She didn't want to meet the man. It was nothing personal. From talking to him on the phone a dozen times, she already knew they'd get on well enough. Ianelli had a telephone voice that would melt butter, a take-charge decisiveness that was rather overwhelming, and a dry sense of humor that tickled her. He'd been polite but also had made it clear that he needed to share an inheritance with a stranger a few thousand miles from his native California the same way he needed a ruptured appendix.

She'd made it clear that she felt the same way. Once probate was settled, he'd proposed the short weekend for both of them to see the place, determine what shape it was in, and set the wheels in motion to sell it. During that telephone conversation more than a month ago, Maggie had sensibly agreed with him. After all, what on earth could she do with half of ninety secluded acres on some godforsaken river in the middle of nowhere? Nothing.

Her plans hadn't changed in the last month and a half, but her life had. Secluded, godforsaken rivers suddenly had an irresistible appeal. Meeting strange men didn't.

Two plane loads of travelers spilled toward the exit doors. A man in a cranberry suit twisted past her, followed by two teenage girls in cropped tight pants and dangling rhinestone earrings. Impatiently Maggie pushed up the sleeve of her green sweater to read the time on her watch. His flight had been due in two hours before hers. So where the devil was he?

Her impatience died like the slam of a freight train, when the first surge of humanity cleared out. There was only one man left standing...by the other Ground Transportation sign.

It definitely wasn't her day.

Rationally, she could care less whether Ianelli was good-looking or a hunchback with crossed eyes. Emotionally, she would have preferred the crossed eyes version. Her lips twisted in wry humor as she reached for the first of her bulky gear.

It was hardly the stranger's fault if he touched off a spring of private pain for Maggie. He was just standing there, doing nothing more offensive than looking like a prime cut of virility. She had nothing against virility, or men in general. It was simply that men with far less impact than Ianelli were the exact reason that godforsaken rivers suddenly had appeal for her.

She probably should have expected that Italian look from his last name. The Latin genes were unmistakable in his broody dark eyes, devil black hair, and skin that naturally bronzed in the sun. Built lean and compact, he radiated a dark energy, like an explosion of impatience and restlessness waiting to happen. His shoulders were an advertisement for concentrated power; he wasn't a man one bumped into by mistake. Correction: women undoubtedly made a point of bumping into him.

From leather aviator jacket to black sweater and jeans, his body language talked up bold, sexy male. Pride echoed in the tilt of a strong chin, the set of his shoulders and the thick shaggy brows that shielded his expression from strangers. And those dark eyes of his never stopped moving. His gaze settled on her slight form briefly, then passed on.

Maggie wasn't surprised. Men were reliably inclined to pass over her in a crowd.

"Ianelli...Mike?" She parked in front of him, and dropped her gear so she could offer him a hand.

Black eyes whisked down to meet hers. Those eyes once and for all explained why the nuns drilled every good Catholic girl to keep a penny between her knees when she kissed. He was "it." Sin. Temptation. All those good things that made up guilt, something Maggie had majored in during her school days.

"You're...Flannery." It was less a question than a statement of acceptance, followed by an imperceptible lessening of tension in his shoulders. His mouth curved in the beginnings of a lazy, relaxed smile.

Both despair and humor settled in Maggie's stomach. She'd seen that exact smile before, it was the kind that a man usually reserved for his favorite niece.

She wasn't sure if it was the spray of freckles on her nose, the bouncy auburn hair that skimmed her shoulders, or a figure that rivaled Audrey Hepburn for curves, but men always took one look and traditionally treated her with affection, courtesy, and respect. On the surface, that was terrific; most women should be so lucky.

Underneath, Maggie had had it with her brand of luck. Her love life could have been rated "G" for general audiences. On the basis of her sexual experiences, she could have auditioned for sainthood. Al, for example, had spent three months treating her as carefully as a soufflé. Only a month ago, in his tactful way, he'd confessed a preference for hot tamales.

Al was not specifically important, except that he'd functioned as a last straw. When Maggie had started counting, there'd been a lot of last straws. There came a time when a woman simply had to accept that a man was never going to look at her the way a woman wanted to be looked at.

And Ianelli's deliberately reassuring smile was sort of salt in the wound. She felt like promising him that she'd gotten the message. She was excellent at picking up those unspoken, ever-friendly, not-interested vibrations from men. *Don't panic, Ianelli,* she thought. *I don't attack strange men, although I have to admit you could bring out the latent reckless streak in a nun.*

Her eyes danced with a woman's private humor; she offered him a smile. "I was getting a little worried when you weren't here—"

"I'm sorry. I meant to meet your plane, but there was a problem with the rental car. Your flight go all right?"

"Fine. Yours?"

"I got in two hours ago—long enough to catch dinner here. Do you need something to eat before we start out?"

"No, they fed us on the plane. Packaged something or other." She made a comical grimace. "I think it was beef. It's hard to be sure. You settled the car problem?"

"Once a little extra cash greased his palms, yes. Nothing to worry about." He hesitated. "No question that we've got a long drive ahead of us. If you want to make a stop first..."

"No, but thanks." She could have had the same conversation with her mother. Except that her mother didn't have those bold eyes, shoulders that never stopped, and chemistry that exuded Dangerous for a two-foot radius. He was a potent brew.

She'd never been susceptible to potent brews, and if she had been, Ianelli's handshake had promised her she was as safe as church. That handshake had been very brisk, very friendly, very over-as-fast-as-possible. "You contacted the caretaker?"

"Yes, for what help that was. We've got a problem with the weather, Maggie..."

Since he was zipping up his jacket, she reached for hers. Her gaze strayed to the width of his muscled chest when he stretched. His eyes—probably just as unconsciously—flickered to her chest, then promptly shifted to her gear. Vaguely she wondered if her entire life might have been different if she'd opted for silicone injections.

Okay, Margaret Mary, she chided herself. This is lots of fun, but let's get serious, shall we? He was easy to talk to; she should be grateful. She concentrated on feeling grateful. "The weather? I could see from the plane it was snowing, but—"

"I'm afraid it's more than snowing. Listen, do you need to pick up any more luggage from the baggage claim?"

"No," she said dryly. A compact sleeping bag sat at his feet, evidently all he felt he needed to survive a weekend. If Maggie left home for more than three hours, she packed close to everything she owned. "What did you mean about the caretaker? Ned . . . ?"

"Whistler. And though he claims the house is in excellent structural shape, he couldn't promise the most ideal living conditions. There's electricity—but only cold water, and I gather the furnace is on the endangered species list. There's no guarantee of heat."

"Knowing how long the house has been empty, I was prepared for no amenities of any kind—hey, you don't have to do that." He'd picked up her duffel bag before she could stop him.

Surprise arched those shaggy brows of his, and then she caught another crack of an indulgent smile. "*How* did you manage to lug this through the airport alone?"

"Willpower," she admitted blithely, and grinned back. To heck with it. Other women might have packed a frothy nightgown for a weekend with a strange man. She'd packed peanut butter, coffee, silverware, a boy scout knife, towel, soap, and bananas. For openers.

She won a husky burst of laughter from him as he moved toward the exit. "After talking with you on the phone, I might have expected you'd be prepared for anything—but Maggie, I think we'd better discuss a change in plans."

"Change in plans? Why?"

But she guessed why, the instant she stepped outside. A howling wind forced freezing air into her lungs. Sleet pelted down in icy nettles, stinging her face and whipping into her hair. Mike grabbed her arm before she could lose her balance. The parking lot was like a skating rink. The lash of wind burned her eyes, making visibility impossible. Philadelphia winters were no bliss, but she'd expected better from this mid-Western state in a melt month. The word here was blizzard.

"Now you know why your plane was a little late." He shouted to be heard over the gale.

"I could see it was snowing—"

"I was told that Indiana's been blessed with the worst winter they've had in years. Five feet of snow this month alone... I'll have you know I left seventy degrees in San Francisco this morning."

She was handed up into a cold leather seat. The door slammed in her ear. She recognized why he'd had a problem with the rental car—he'd exchanged their prearranged sedan for a four-wheel-drive vehicle. When Michael climbed into the other side, she was fiercely rubbing her hands together. He started the engine, then flicked on the defroster, windshield wipers, and heater.

The engine had no intention of warming up too fast, which gave Maggie a chance to catch her breath and pretend she wasn't affected by having been sandwiched to Michael's side for that mad dash through the parking lot. Never mind sleet, storm and dead of night, her right thigh still bore the imprint of his left one. Are you really determined to be silly about this, Margaret Mary? said a voice inside her head.

It seemed she was. She was enjoying being silly, actually. The zippy little traces of lust sizzling through her system were unexpected, totally out of character, and darned fun. For years she'd specialized in being "good." Maybe it took getting completely away from her normal life to feel daring and a little reckless and somewhat foolish. She'd been beginning to doubt her ability to feel woman feelings, sexual feelings.

It wasn't as if he would ever know she was attracted to him. Mike's easy conversation and manner had made it clear she was no more than a rival for his kid sister, and that was fine by Maggie. She didn't need two days stuck with an awkward stranger.

"About that change in plans," he said quietly. "I can only guess what road conditions are, but they can't be good. If you want to be set up in a motel for the night, I could go on to the house and pick you up in the morning."

"Thank you, but no," she said swiftly.

He hesitated. "I didn't meant to imply that I would make any decisions without you. Obviously, we've both got to agree on what to do with the place, but there'll be adequate time for you to see it in daylight...."

"Yes."

"The weather is a bitch...."

"It certainly is."

"And if the expense of a motel is a problem—"

"Ianelli," she said gently, "Forget it. I'm going."

For a moment there was utter quiet, just the rhythm of windshield wipers trying to conquer a ceaseless driving sleet. Then Mike abruptly shoved the car in gear, and moments later, they were on the road. "Did you by any chance inherit a slight streak of stubbornness from your grandfather?" he asked dryly.

She leaned her head back, well aware Ianelli would have preferred to stash her in the nearest motel and that most women probably wouldn't have argued with him—about anything. "The grandfather I inherited my half of our white elephant from? No, he wasn't stubborn. But he did teach me to play poker at age five and fed me my first shot of whiskey when I was seven. Anyone in the family could tell you that he was a totally irresponsible man."

Mike said quietly, "You loved him."

"I adored him," she corrected, and left it at that. There was a core of Maggie no one touched. Gramps was part of that.

Gramps's letter to her was still in her purse. Most of it she knew by heart: *I would have sold the place years ago, if it hadn't been for a redheaded child with too-serious green eyes who used to climb on my lap and listen to an old man dream. You and I are the only ones who still believe in treasure, Maggie. It's there, waiting for you.*

As a little girl, Maggie had believed in rainbows, treasures, and her grandfather...not necessarily in that order. At twenty-five, she was naturally an older, wiser breed. But that letter still warmed her heart and reminded her of a time in her life when she believed she could touch the sky, embrace the world, exult in the wind on a summer day.

She no longer believed in treasures, and realistically she hadn't built up any serious expectations about this inheritance. At her heart's level, though, she desperately wanted something back that she seemed to have lost. The yearning was nothing she could name, but it was still real.

The craziest anticipation kept building as Mike drove. Few other cars were braving the weather conditions; they might as well have been alone on the road. The snow swallowed them in silence, making landmarks all but impossible to identify. Each mile seemed to be taking her farther and farther from her life and away from everything that was safe and familiar. She felt anticipation and anxiety, fear and exhilaration. She couldn't shake the feeling that coming here was right, that something was waiting for her.

Almost two hours later, Michael turned off the highway. The new road was suddenly less illuminated, more difficult to drive. Blinding white flew past them against a night blacker than ebony velvet.

"Going to sleep on me, Maggie?"

She turned her head. "No...I just thought you didn't need conversation, trying to drive in conditions like this. For that matter, I'm used to winter driving, so if you want me to take a turn at the wheel—"

"No, but thanks."

She smiled, expecting the answer.

"You're warm enough?"

"Fine," she assured him.

"This heater isn't the best." He leaned over to adjust the blower.

"As a navigator, I'm certainly failing on the job. I haven't once asked you if you wanted some help locating roads—"

"Whistler sent me a good set of directions." He whisked her a glance for just a few seconds when his luminous black eyes focused on her. She thought absently that a woman could lose herself in those eyes, and the man was just giving her a polite glance.

He seemed to invite casual conversation, and Maggie gave it to him, sensing he wanted the small talk to help keep him alert. From the beginning of this venture, they'd opted for a division of labor. She'd handled the legal nonsense regarding wills, probate and deeds; he'd made contact with the caretaker and managed the arrangements for this meeting. In the process, neither had come across any information that made sense out of their shared inheritance. The Flannerys were from Philadelphia; the Ianellis strictly West Coast. Why or how or for what purpose their mutual grandfathers had happened to ally in another generation was a total mystery.

The mystery fascinated Maggie, but the man next to her increasingly interested her more. As they talked, she studied him. The on and off gash of distant streetlights illuminated his strong profile and the gleam of his thick, dark hair. At first glance, she hadn't noticed the brooding lines of strain and weariness etched on his brow. She noticed them now. She also found that he concentrated conversation only on impersonal subjects, and that his lazy voice was a total contrast to the tension in his long brown hands on the wheel. He sat very still, apparently a self-contained man in perfect control.

The tension in his hands and the look in his eyes said something else. It took Maggie forever before she finally isolated what she saw in him—anger. Old anger, not new. The man had learned a long time ago to control his expressions, to cloak pride in a slash of a smile, to divert a woman from coming too close with a sexy tenor designed to melt blood, stir hormones, ignite wanton fantasies.

The man *did* radiate sex appeal. Maggie had already written off her private attraction as hopeless, but the instinct to want to reach out and touch him at another level entirely was almost automatic. She understood trouble; she had it. And if caring was something she shouldn't rationally feel for a stranger, it wasn't a rational kind of night.

The darkness kept coming, the pure white snow, the endless silence.

"What's the sudden smile for?"

She turned her head, and propped her foot on the dash. "I think it's beginning to get to me."

"What is?"

"All this." She motioned to the night. "It's rather Hitchcockian, don't you think? I mean—a dark night, a lonely road, strangers. Going to a house that hasn't been lived in for almost fifty years, with a mysterious history of treasure—"

"You never believed that nonsense?"

"Of course not," Maggie said smoothly. She'd originally told him about that part of her grandfather's letter because she felt she had to. Anything found in the house was obviously theirs, not just hers. His response had been a short bark of laughter and a promise that she could keep whatever gold bullion and diamonds they found. At the time she'd laughed, too. That was before Al, before an unfortunately fragile woman's ego had been shattered yet again, before she'd sat herself down and faced facts about herself and men.

If love had been ruthlessly crossed off her list, there had to be something else. It wasn't exactly the treasure she was counting on...but something to reach for and hold on to. Way back she'd had dreams of living in the country, of owning something that was strictly her own. Where on earth had all the dreams gone?

"Maggie, if there'd been anything valuable in the house, my own grandfather would have claimed his share years ago. He died stone broke—and even if the old codgers had left something, it would be gone by now. The house has been vandalized twice in the last few years."

"The caretaker told you that?"

Mike nodded. "Nothing serious, just kids' pranks. The kind of thing that's inevitable in a house left empty for too long." He paused. "On the phone, you certainly never indicated you felt any sentiment for the place."

"No. How could I? It was nothing I shared with my grandfather. I didn't even know it existed."

He seemed to choose his words carefully. "So nothing's changed. All we're going to do is assess it, judge what repairs have to be done to sell it, and set that potential sale in motion."

"Absolutely," she concurred.

"So you're not going to spring any notions about suddenly wanting to keep the property, are you?"

Maggie didn't allow herself to hesitate. "Are you kidding? I can't even make my rent payments. I'm just talking about momentary mental apparitions. Brought on by the dark night—"

"Strangers, and a lonely road that seems to be going nowhere." The faint, indulgent smile didn't quite meet his eyes. "From talking to you on the phone, I think I expected a totally practical, efficient—"

"Sensible woman?" Maggie asked dryly. "You can stop worrying, Ianelli. I hold down a job as an Assistant Product Manager. True, it's a position that requires a certain amount of insanity to function—but I can also give you character references as to how efficient and practical I am. And my family's the flamboyant bunch, not me. If you asked them, they'd be happy to tell you that I'm the only stabilizing influence in the clan. Now does that sound like a woman who's suddenly going to spring off and go stark raving mad for a stand of woods and a shack somewhere in the middle of Indiana?"

She meant him to laugh. He did. She'd wanted to hear him laugh, wondered how the look of laughter would change his expression, and she had, for those few short seconds, an image of a very different man. Relaxed, his dark eyes sparkled pure devilment. His natural smile was sensual and easy. The taut lines of strain on his brow disappeared.

The secret of him, the mystery of him, only deepened for Maggie. "You know," she said lightly, "in all those phone conversations we had, all we discussed was lawyers and white elephants and the logistics of handling this weekend. I never thought to ask you if you had to arrange this time away around a family."

"No."

He didn't say it unkindly, but the short answer should have carried its own message. It did, actually, but Maggie tried one more time to find common ground, her tone deliberately friendly and nothing more. "I never even thought to ask you what you did for a living."

"Check the map one last time, would you? I think we're close to the last turnoff."

She took the map from the dashboard, which she couldn't possibly see without X-ray vision, and accepted the diversion for what it was. Don't pry, goose. She felt like saying, Don't be silly, Ianelli. That dark brooding is incredibly sexy, but completely wasted on me. I'm not going to intrude on your life. I'm not even going to see you again after these two days.

She shot him a glance, thought that the dark brooding wasn't actually *entirely* wasted on her, and then leaned back with her eyes closed. A fantasy popped into her mind, of a cougar backed into a corner, lean and dangerous and fierce, prepared to fight for his own no matter what the odds. The cougar had Mike's eyes. In the fantasy, she leaned forward to pet him, and the cougar turned from fierce to tender and arched for the touch of her hand.

Maggie mentally sighed. Her daydream was not only ridiculous but corny. Whatever seemed to be wrong with her lately was getting worse. Proximity to this stranger wasn't helping. Actually, the nearness to Mike seemed to accelerate yearnings that had no rational basis, needs that had no name.

Her eyes shot open when the car jolted over a bump.

"You're strapped in?" Mike's voice was suddenly terse.

"Yes," she lied. She wasn't, but she clapped the two bits of metal together in short order.

The last road was an ice-covered, pot-holed horror. Low-hanging branches whipped at the windows on both sides. Moments later they crossed a narrow stone bridge that was a mirror glaze of ice. Maggie didn't know when she'd seen the last streetlight, but was suddenly aware there were none. A pit-black sky backdropped a blinding white glare of snow. The ground was simply white and more white, the road had no perimeters and there blew a ceaseless driving wind. She thought the headlights illuminated a tall rusty wrought iron gate in the distance, but there was no way to be sure.

Fear curled inside her and mixed with a shiver of exhilaration. The night was alive, waiting. Her tame quiet life might have been centuries behind her and it didn't matter; it was no longer relevant. Her palms were suddenly slick. The small lick of fear, the tense feeling of exhilaration—that was now.

"If I had any sense, I'd take you right back to a motel."

Mike's voice was grim and angry. Maggie wasn't paying attention. It couldn't be much farther. He couldn't continue to drive in conditions like this, and she couldn't believe there was anything remotely livable within miles.

And then, suddenly, they were there. The palest light flickering through snow grew brighter. Mike braked beneath the yard light, peered out, and then just looked at her. "Hitchcock enough for you?" he asked dryly.

She climbed out of the car, uncaring of the cold and biting wind. Ahead of them was a monster of a house. A square two-story home in solid stone, with a shadowed veranda that surrounded the first floor. Snow tucked into the corners of oblong black windows. Second-story iron balconies jutted over the river, which was so close that Maggie could hear the surge of water splashing against the icy shore.

Her breath caught, held. She'd been led to expect a house in a country setting, nothing more. She'd never expected this. Huge maples and oaks surrounded the place, their naked branches coated with ice like long crystal fingers that shivered in the wind. Shadows played under the yellow yard light left on for them. No other buildings were in sight. No footprints marred the swirls and mounds of endless, ice-topped snow.

Ghosts belonged in the place. Ghosts and princesses, legends and dungeons...

"Lord, don't tell me. You like it." Mike was reaching in the back of the car, slinging gear over his shoulders. Maggie turned, then rushed belatedly to help him. "Don't—I can manage. Just watch your step on the way to the door."

His fingers suddenly closed on her arm, and when she looked up, his dark eyes pinned hers. "Flannery, if this place is no more habitable than it looks—"

"Yes, I know. We'll go back to a motel," she said gently. She knew, if he didn't, that he wasn't braving another two hours of driving conditions like the ones they'd just encountered.

"I mean it."

"Yes."

Since she was agreeing with him, she had no idea why his jaw suddenly tightened. When he released her arm, she tried to look sensible, practical, efficient. She tried to smile.

"Maggie..."

She didn't know what he wanted to say, but she'd already turned away, was staring at the house again. Even if her entire life weren't in Philadelphia, that first glance told her she didn't have the capital to fix the place or maintain it. And what on earth could she possibly do with such a sprawling monstrosity even if she could afford it? Nothing had changed.

Only everything had changed. Ah, Gramps, she thought fleetingly, how could you do this to me? The house could have been a fishing cottage, a ramshackle falling down shack. Maybe she could have gone back then, back to her life, back to being plain old Maggie.

Only the house was her oldest daydream in living technicolor: country, privacy, fresh air and the space to pursue something uniquely her own.

One look told her she'd never be able to give it up.

Two

___

"Mike, I just can't *believe* it!"

Maggie was waiting on the porch steps for him to produce a key. Shivering like mad, her shoulders were hunched inside her jacket. Her eyes were as bright as green crystals, her red mouth all but trembling... but not with cold.

She was *not* the lady that more than a dozen rational phone calls had led Mike to expect.

Climbing the six steps up to the veranda, he dropped the two sleeping bags and dug into his pocket. "I'll have the key in a second."

"No hurry—and I should have helped you carry everything, darn it."

"No problem." His palm discovered the key; he stuck it into the old brass lock and turned it. Maggie snatched both of their sleeping bags and rushed in. Mike followed more slowly, his eyes landing on the neatly stacked wood by the door.

"Ianelli! There's no—"

He found the first light switch, and was rewarded twice. First because Whistler hadn't lied when he said the electricity worked, and second, with one of Maggie's smiles. At first glance, he'd thought her plain. Until she smiled.

Abruptly she perched her hands on her hips, five feet one inch of daunting energy. "All right," she said briskly. "I don't know what you think we should do first—"

He couldn't imagine who she thought she was fooling. "I think you should explore," he said with equal gravity.

"But if you—"

"Flannery, there was no way we were ever going to do anything tonight but settle in. You can't check out plumbing and electrical systems at this time of night."

"Well..."

He watched. Her pace was mature and sedate until she was out of sight, and then the click-click of her heeled boots raced across bare floors. In the meantime, her jacket had been sloughed off by the door, and a single white wool glove was carelessly discarded by a window.

He'd anticipated an intelligent, reasonable young woman with a rational head on her shoulders. He'd expected the easy humor and the natural friendliness and the bubble of energy that was exactly how she'd come across on the phone. He'd even expected she'd be the chew-the-nails type as she was.

He hadn't envisioned luminescent green eyes, the fragile sensitive features, the silky flyaway hair that framed her face and never looked quite brushed. He hadn't envisioned the whimsical smiles, the imagination, the life that vibrated from her.

That changed nothing. He didn't want her here. He could have handled this whole business in half the time alone. The shared inheritance forced a short alliance, but "short" was the operative word for Mike. He didn't want to be around a woman. Any woman.

He dragged a weary hand through his hair, his practical eye automatically cataloging electrical sockets, heating ducts, the condition of floors and ceilings. Whistler had given him a written report, but Mike never trusted anyone's judgment but his own. His mind skimmed a dozen details, assessing, evaluating, questioning, yet he found himself half listening for the sound of her voice.

Her voice was annoying. Clear and sweet, oddly low for a woman as slight as she was, and distracting.

Mike was not easily distracted. Shedding his jacket, he bent down to check the fireplace flue, and scrounged in his pocket for matches. He struck the flame, and when the pale thread of smoke soared up the chimney, he blew out the match, stood back up and went outside to bring in kindling and logs. Pain suddenly flowed through him like cold clear water. Private pain, a familiar, gnawing ache.

Five months before, he'd been fired. And there hadn't been an hour in all those long months when he could seem to forget that.

At thirty-one he'd been the youngest chief financial officer that Stuart-Spencer's had ever had. He didn't regret the loss of the job. He'd found a man on the take and chosen to act on that; his mistake was in not guessing that his boss was on the same take...or that finding another position would be impossible when his references had been blackballed.

The slur on his honesty haunted him. Coming from a wild clan who occasionally strayed on the wrong side of the law, Mike was inordinately sensitive about his personal honesty and integrity. He never tolerated even white lies. He was also proud.

And getting damn close to broke. Ostensibly this inheritance was a windfall, but it wasn't a windfall Mike wanted or needed. He wanted nothing from anyone that he hadn't earned on his own. The property taxes, the wages of the caretaker, and the repairs it would take to make this place salable, Mike saw only as a drain on cash he didn't have, and a distraction on time that should be spent job hunting. There was nothing permanent for him in a house on some damned river in Indiana.

"Mike, I don't believe this!"

He turned, but all he caught was a slash of vibrant green eyes before she was gone again. Wariness etched a frown between his brows. He didn't need the complication of Maggie forming an attachment to the house. Maggie herself was like an annoying splash of color in a world that had been bitter gray for months.

He didn't need or want the color. He wanted to be alone.

Maggie blew a strand of hair from her cheek. She was trying to judge the house rationally, but it was so hard. The downstairs was built around a wide staircase. There was a parlor and another parlor and an empty library and rooms that seemed to have no purpose, all partitioned by French doors. Cobwebs hung from the corners and the dust on the floors was an inch thick.

Neither cobwebs nor dust mattered. Maggie hugged her arms around herself, calling out marvel after marvel to Mike. Such unexpected riches! Several chandeliers were solid brass, two were crystal. Real crystal. Two rooms had fireplaces with marble hearths. Crushed gold velvet draperies still hung from the windows, trimmed with fringed tassels, impossibly faded, still marvelously elegant.

A hodgepodge of furniture was still strewn here and there. A fringed lamp sat in the middle of one room. In another, she found two wingback couches in burgundy velvet, and in the far room off the river, she found the strangest tables—semi-circular, waist high, and covered with stained green felt.

"Mike, would you look at this? I can't imagine what these were used for..."

The kitchen was at the very back of the house. The pantry was bigger than her bedroom at home, and the cook stove looked six feet wide. A window on one of the inside walls opened and closed like a cashier's window at a bank. Was it used to help serve people in the main dining room? She opened a second inside window, and discovered a dumb waiter system with a rope and pulley system still attached. "Ianelli! What on *earth* are you doing? You have to see this!"

She rushed on, letting her hands glide on the mahogany banister as she raced up the staircase. At the top, breathless, she fumbled for a light switch. It took a moment to find it, and when she did her brows arched in surprise.

There were more than a dozen bedrooms, and for some reason all but one bedroom door had been numbered in delicate golf leaf. The first she stepped into revealed a tarnished brass bed, a bare mattress, faded scarlet draperies in raw silk, and walls painted a garish red.

The next bedroom was a shocking pink, the next lavender, another emerald, another red, white and blue. The color schemes were rather startling after the muted, tasteful elegance on the first floor. A shocking thought occurred to her. She tried to banish it.

"Maggie, you're all right?" Mike called up from below.

"Fine." But her tone was suddenly distracted.

"What's wrong?"

She paced back to the stairs to peer over the open banister. "Why should anything be wrong?"

1. How do you rate _____
   (Please print book TITLE)

   1.6 ☐ excellent   .4 ☐ good   .2 ☐ not so good
   .5 ☐ very good   .3 ☐ fair   .1 ☐ poor

2. How likely are you to purchase another book:

   in this *series* ?   by this *author* ?
   2.1 ☐ definitely would purchase   3.1 ☐ definitely would purchase
   .2 ☐ probably would puchase   .2 ☐ probably would puchase
   .3 ☐ probably would not purchase   .3 ☐ probably would not purchase
   .4 ☐ definitely would not purchase   .4 ☐ definitely would not purchase

3. How does this book compare with similar books you usually read?

   4.1 ☐ far better than others   .2 ☐ better than others   .3 ☐ about the
   .4 ☐ not as good   .5 ☐ definitely not as good   same

4. Please check the statements you feel best describe this book.

   5. ☐ Easy to read   6. ☐ Too much violence/anger
   7. ☐ Realistic conflict   8. ☐ Wholesome/not too sexy
   9. ☐ Too sexy   10. ☐ Interesting characters
   11. ☐ Original plot   12. ☐ Especially romantic
   13. ☐ Not enough humor   14. ☐ Difficult to read
   15. ☐ Didn't like the subject 16. ☐ Good humor in story
   17. ☐ Too predictable   18. ☐ Not enough description of setting
   19. ☐ Believable characters   20. ☐ Fast paced
   21. ☐ Couldn't put the book down 22. ☐ Heroine too juvenile/weak/silly
   23. ☐ Made me feel good   24. ☐ Too many foreign/unfamiliar words
   25. ☐ Hero too dominating   26. ☐ Too wholesome/not sexy enough
   27. ☐ Not enough romance   28. ☐ Liked the setting
   29. ☐ Ideal hero   30. ☐ Heroine too independent
   31. ☐ Slow moving   32. ☐ Unrealistic conflict
   33. ☐ Not enough suspense   34. ☐ Sensuous/not too sexy
   35. ☐ Liked the subject   36. ☐ Too much description of setting

5. What *most* prompted you to buy this book?

   37. ☐ Read others in series   38. ☐ Title   39. ☐ Cover art
   40. ☐ Friend's recommendation 41. ☐ Author   42. ☐ In-store display
   43. ☐ TV, radio or magazine ad 44. ☐ Price   45. ☐ Story outline
   46. ☐ Ad inside other books   47. ☐ Other _____ (please specify)

6. Please indicate how many romance paperbacks you read in a month.

   48.1 ☐ 1 to 4   .2 ☐ 5 to 10   .3 ☐ 11 to 15   .4 ☐ more than 15

7. Please indicate your sex and age group.

   49.1 ☐ Male   50.1 ☐ under 15   .3 ☐ 25-34   .5 ☐ 50-64
   .2 ☐ Female   .2 ☐ 15-24   .4 ☐ 35-49   .6 ☐ 65 or older

8. Have you any additional comments about this book?

   _____ (51)
   _____ (53)

Thank you for completing and returning this questionnaire.

NAME _____

ADDRESS _____
(Please Print)

CITY _____

ZIP CODE _____

BUSINESS REPLY MAIL

FIRST CLASS   PERMIT NO. 717   BUFFALO, NY

POSTAGE WILL BE PAID BY ADDRESSEE

NATIONAL READER SURVEYS

901 Fuhrmann Blvd.
P.O. Box 1395
Buffalo, N.Y. 14240-9961

1. How do you rate _____
   (Please print book TITLE)

   1.6 ☐ excellent   .4 ☐ good   .2 ☐ not so good
   .5 ☐ very good   .3 ☐ fair   .1 ☐ poor

IA

2. How likely are you to purchase another book:

   in this *series* ?   by this *author* ?

   2.1 ☐ definitely would purchase   3.1 ☐ definitely would purchase
   .2 ☐ probably would puchase   .2 ☐ probably would puchase
   .3 ☐ probably would not purchase   .3 ☐ probably would not purchase
   .4 ☐ definitely would not purchase   .4 ☐ definitely would not purchase

3. How does this book compare with similar books you usually read?

   4.1 ☐ far better than others   .2 ☐ better than others   .3 ☐ about the
   .4 ☐ not as good   .5 ☐ definitely not as good   same

4. Please check the statements you feel best describe this book.

   5. ☐ Easy to read   6. ☐ Too much violence/anger
   7. ☐ Realistic conflict   8. ☐ Wholesome/not too sexy
   9. ☐ Too sexy   10. ☐ Interesting characters
   11. ☐ Original plot   12. ☐ Especially romantic
   13. ☐ Not enough humor   14. ☐ Difficult to read
   15. ☐ Didn't like the subject   16. ☐ Good humor in story
   17. ☐ Too predictable   18. ☐ Not enough description of setting
   19. ☐ Believable characters   20. ☐ Fast paced
   21. ☐ Couldn't put the book down   22. ☐ Heroine too juvenile/weak/silly
   23. ☐ Made me feel good   24. ☐ Too many foreign/unfamiliar words
   25. ☐ Hero too dominating   26. ☐ Too wholesome/not sexy enough
   27. ☐ Not enough romance   28. ☐ Liked the setting
   29. ☐ Ideal hero   30. ☐ Heroine too independent
   31. ☐ Slow moving   32. ☐ Unrealistic conflict
   33. ☐ Not enough suspense   34. ☐ Sensuous/not too sexy
   35. ☐ Liked the subject   36. ☐ Too much description of setting

5. What *most* prompted you to buy this book?

   37. ☐ Read others in series   38. ☐ Title   39. ☐ Cover art
   40. ☐ Friend's recommendation   41. ☐ Author   42. ☐ In-store display
   43. ☐ TV, radio or magazine ad   44. ☐ Price   45. ☐ Story outline
   46. ☐ Ad inside other books   47. ☐ Other _____ (please specify)

6. Please indicate how many romance paperbacks you read in a month.

   48.1 ☐ 1 to 4   .2 ☐ 5 to 10   .3 ☐ 11 to 15   .4 ☐ more than 15

7. Please indicate your sex and age group.

   49.1 ☐ Male   50.1 ☐ under 15   .3 ☐ 25-34   .5 ☐ 50-64
   .2 ☐ Female   .2 ☐ 15-24   .4 ☐ 35-49   .6 ☐ 65 or older

8. Have you any additional comments about this book?

   _____ (51)
   _____ (53)

Thank you for completing and returning this questionnaire.

PRINTED IN U.S.A.

"You stopped shouting," he said dryly.

Her eyes danced. She was touched that he'd checked on her. He looked quite irritated, as if regretting the impulse. Maggie was momentarily mesmerized by the natural male arrogance of hands on lean hips, legs apart, snapping black eyes. A most irreverent thought popped into her mind, that she wouldn't mind being leaned against a wall, layered against those hips, those legs, those hands, that mouth. Flannery, behave. She sighed mentally. "I've been shouting, have I?"

"Only about every thirty seconds, give or take."

"Don't you ever behave like a kid, Ianelli?"

"No."

It disturbed her, that he meant it. "Pity." She added teasingly, "I can walk sedately through the rest of the house like a nun going to vespers, if a little enthusiasm upsets you."

"Don't give me a hard time, Flannery. I don't care if you shout from here to doomsday. But when you stopped calling out, I had these visions of you fallen through floorboards or locked up in the attic or—"

He stopped talking abruptly, glared at her and disappeared from sight. Maggie straightened thoughtfully. The man was almost as much of a mystery as the house... but for the moment, she had the upstairs to finish exploring.

The bathroom was a giant of a room with two small locking cubicles marked LADIES and GENTS. The main space contained a pink porcelain tub built on a two step pedestal, an expansive vanity in Italian marble, and a delicate gold and prismed chandelier hang-

ing over the tub. Maggie rubbed the bridge of her nose
with a finger, staring at the chandelier. Where she
came from, chandeliers didn't traditionally hang over
bathtubs.

Perhaps right about now we'd better face that
Gramps didn't exactly operate your average run of the
mill business, Margaret Mary. The last bedroom she
walked into confirmed those suspicions.

The last bedroom was secluded at the far end of the
hall. Windowed on three sides, the room jutted over
the river. There were steps leading down from a private balcony, making the room accessible from the
outside but as far as Maggie could tell, those steps led
to nothing but the water. She might have been more
curious about that, if the rest of the room hadn't cap-
tivated her attention.

If vandals had bothered the rest of the house, they
thankfully hadn't been in here. Pale blue draperies
canopied a double bed in folds of shadowy silk, à la
Arabian nights. A loveseat in powder-blue brocade
was echoed in the mirrored wall behind it. Where the
other floors had been varnished wood, this room was
carpeted in thick, luxurious wool. Pure white, albeit
now dusty. The window seat was covered in faded
satin cushions.

It was the room of a very sensual woman. A woman
who loved textures, who reveled in the senses, who
took her creature comforts very seriously.

There was no need for a number on the door, Maggie thought fleetingly. The madam's room was unmistakable.

She went down the stairs at half the speed she'd taken to go up. Below, a fire was blazing in the marble hearth in the room closest to the kitchen. Two armloads of logs were stacked by the fireplace, doors had been closed to seal off the heat, and Mike had dragged the two couches in, close to the warmth.

Crouched on his haunches, he was feeding the flames. Firelight played on his strong features when he turned to look at her, and she could hardly miss the devil's smile. He knew.

"I don't know if you noticed those strange looking tables in the other room—" she started hesitantly.

"Casino tables."

"I think, unfortunately, that I guessed that." Her head whipped around, searching for her duffel bag. Mike had stashed it with the other gear by the foot of the stairs. She tugged it close to the couch, dropped to the seat, and unzipped it.

Bananas emerged first. Mike caught the bag of cashews she tossed him. Raisins made their way to the seat next to her, then bags of dried fruit. A cellophane-wrapped container of coffee, then spoons. She dug farther. A moment later she drew out two paper cups with trivia questions on them, and a sterling silver flask.

"Maggie?" He was still recovering from watching her unpack.

The potent smell of rich, strong Irish whiskey filled the air as she poured the gold liquid into the cups. When she handed him his, he saw the faintest coral sweep her cheekbones, but the laughter in her eyes was unmistakable. "Don't you think we'd better toast inheriting this den of iniquity, Ianelli?"

He said gravely, "I think we should toast your ability to pack everything but the kitchen sink in one small duffel bag."

"That, too, then."

He smothered a laugh when she leaned forward to click paper cups with him. "To the den?" he suggested.

"To the den," she agreed, took a sip, and shivered all over. "To grandfathers." They toasted again, and then she promoted, "Might as well make one to sin in general, since that's apparently what this estate specialized in."

That time he did laugh. Her lips pursed like a persimmon every time she took a swallow. "Your favorite drink?" he said dryly.

"I've hated whiskey since I was seven."

"Then why on earth did you bring it?"

"Because I usually get insomnia sleeping away from home. A shot of whiskey before bed—or at least the threat of having to swallow one—helps that." She pushed off her boots, and curled up on the couch with her feet under her. "I'm waiting for the horror to hit," she confessed ruefully.

"You're upset because of your grandfather?"

She sighed. "I realized the house was built in 1930, but I certainly never made the association to bootlegging times. Suddenly a few clues drop into place—like why no one in the family knew about it. Only it's still hard to reconcile my image of Gramps with a man who ran liquor, gambling and women during prohibition times.''

"He would have been very young, Maggie," Mike said quietly. He crossed to the opposite couch and sank down. "My grandfather was equally young, with a family of relatives financially dependent on him when the market crashed in 1929."

She looked at him curiously. "You loved your grandfather? You were close?"

She knew the minute she asked that she'd scaled that invisible wall of his privacy again. For a moment, she thought he wasn't going to answer. "I loved him," Mike said shortly. "But we argued. When I was a little kid, he was the one man I respected above any other. We parted ways over an issue of integrity. With my grandfather, family came first. In his business life, if he had to lie, cheat or steal to provide the best for them . . .'' Mike shrugged, and motioned to the room around them. "None of this surprises me, not where my grandfather was concerned. So don't assume your grandfather was solely responsible."

She fell silent, wanting to ask him questions and not daring to. If he'd opened up for those few short seconds, it was for her . . . to shield her from unpleasant truths about Gramps. His kindness touched her. "I still can't imagine how they ever met," she said finally.

"I doubt we'll ever know that."

"Or why they left it to us. My Gramps had four children, all living when he died. A zillion grandchildren..." She thought of her grandfather's letter to her, and fell silent again.

"I don't have any answers for you, Flannery." Mike finished the whiskey in one long gulp, then surged up restlessly to tend the fire again. The truth was, as soon as he'd realized what the place was, he had a good idea why Joe Ianelli had left him his half.

The rift between grandfather and grandson had troubled Mike for years, and when the old man died it was on Mike's conscience. Joe had accused him of being rigid, unbending in principle, a man lacking compassion. Integrity wasn't a God. Honesty was the most easily jettisoned cargo on the ship of survival.

There was no possible way Mike could agree, but it was like the old man's ironic sense of humor to have the last word in an argument in the form of this inheritance. Money had been made here by dishonest means, which went against Mike's even grain. That same money had made it possible for a cocky young Italian to support a family of immigrant relatives during the depression. In his mind, he could see the old man's face again. *You think you can get away with seeing everything in black and white? To hell with you for judging me.*

His mouth formed a dry smile as he remembered his response. *Dammit, I never judged you, Joe. I loved you. I just chose to live my life differently. Believe me, I'm paying the price for the feelings I have about integrity.*

A log snapped in the fireplace, and a spray of sparks illuminated the fine lines around his eyes and mouth.

Maggie's eyes were drawn to his mouth, to the way his chin was dusted with a night beard. The flames made his hair look like wet ink and no man's eyes had a right to be that compelling. His dark skin was taut over strong bones, giving him a fierce look, the appearance of a man who was only tamed on the surface. She looked at him and saw mystery. She looked at him and saw depths a woman could get lost in.

No man like him had ever passed through her life, however fleetingly. She didn't want to be caught staring at him, but couldn't seem to help it. He might as well have worn a sign on his forehead that said "Forbidden To Women Like Margaret Mary."

A grown woman should know better than to indulge in forbidden fantasies. She normally did. But the house itself wasn't helping. Every time she closed her eyes she could see images of elegant women in flapper dresses with satin fringe and long ropes of pearls and men in tuxedos behind casino tables. She heard low-voiced sultry laughter and the clink of champagne glasses....

She kept waiting for a little moral horror to settle in regarding her grandfather's illegal business. That didn't happen since the house had no cold-blooded atmosphere of exploitation. The opposite was true; the aura was all of wicked but romantic images. She imagined how it was. The glitter of lights off the river, marble and satins and silks, French perfume, silk stockings with seams and high, high heels and men with dangerous eyes. The women she pictured were of another age, a sexually repressed age, and it was so easy for Maggie to understand how difficult a woman might have found those rules to live by. But she wouldn't have had to here. Here she could have brazenly chosen a life-style that included sexual choices: she could have coaxed a man upstairs if she wanted to and wouldn't if she chose not to; she could have reached for personal freedom and done it in an atmosphere of wealth and glamor and luxury.

Her gaze wandered helplessly back to Mike. She knew she was making something pretty out of something that might not have been that way at all. It didn't stop the rush of fantasies from coming, and with his dark looks and brooding eyes, Mike was part of the fantasy. He could have been a bootlegger, tough and sexy, living on the fringe of the law. He would look elegant in a tuxedo. He had the look of a man who'd never lived by anyone's rules but his own, a man who liked risks . . . and women.

"Maggie, what's the rest of your family like?"

Her eyelashes shuttered down instantly. She reached casually for a bag of dried fruit, and placed an apricot between her lips. "Colorful," she said lightly. "They've all got wild red hair and incredible style. My mother lives for the theater. My oldest sister's on her third husband." She grinned. "I have an aunt who was once a stripper. She didn't do it for money. Just for kicks, if that tells you anything about her."

She wouldn't have kept talking, if he hadn't coaxed her with lazy, easy questions. She made him chuckle when she told him that the crazy Flannery clan had popped her into a private Catholic girl's school because she was their last chance for a saint. That her family had been determined that she live a normal life, behave by an intelligent set of rules, and specialize in humdrum.

"Those are tough ambitions for a woman to live up to," she said with a cheeky grin, and earned his husky laughter again. She badly wanted his laughter, wanted to be honest with him. Surely the sexual vibrations she felt would disappear if they laughed together?

But his laughter was kind, gentle, a sharing thing. It didn't help. "Maggie, the last thing you are is humdrum," he scolded gently.

"How little you know." She reached for another apricot, let her teeth sink into it. "But then there was Gramps," she said absently. "Gramps didn't think much of humdrum. Gramps was my escape valve. Not that he wasn't as crazy as all of them, but his dreams came from inside of him. If you listened to him, you'd believe in the moon, too. He was always reaching...."

Mike listened. Maggie was funny and open and ruthlessly honest about herself. His own personal problems faded for that hour. He heard tales of her childhood and of her family and heard the voice of a woman who was determined not to be a dreamer...and clearly was. Mike couldn't think of a time he'd ever run across a woman quite like her. He found himself oddly irritated when she tried to stop talking.

Originally, he'd only started the conversation for her sake. Hopefully, friendly chatter would dispel the quiet little looks she occasionally sneaked his way.

Mike wasn't blind. He knew she was attracted to him. Maggie's eyes hid nothing.

He had no women in his life—a man without a job or future had nothing to offer. Loneliness came with his particular brand of integrity, and he accepted that. But if he had been tempted it would never be a woman like Maggie. All his adult life, he'd only sought lovers who were as honest about life as he was. Mutual needs made up commitment, not the gloss of love words.

He knew intuitively that Maggie still believed in the gloss of love words. Those sudden flashes of emerald in her eyes half amused him, half annoyed him. She was twenty-five, and should be old enough to have a protective veneer over that first vulnerable layer. Someone was going to hurt her sometime.

It wasn't going to be him. In spite of himself, Mike was a little touched she looked at him that certain way. She was vulnerable... few women struck him as truly vulnerable these days. Protective urges that he didn't know he had, prickled warningly. For two days, he could guarantee she'd be safe with him.

When she hid a sleepy yawn behind her hand, Mike used it as an excuse to stand up and stretch. "It's past midnight, did you realize? I think it's time we both settled in. It'll be a long day tomorrow." He moved toward the fire. "I don't know how cold it is upstairs, but if you want to set up on one of these couches by the fire—"

"No, really, I'll be fine upstairs. It isn't that cold and my sleeping bag's made of down." Maggie didn't want him coming across her in the morning still asleep, looking like a cat had been in her hair. Springing to her feet, she rezipped her duffel tote and then glanced around for her sleeping bag. "Mike? You might be prepared for a rather wild assortment of bedrooms upstairs. As in pink, scarlet, emerald—"

"The green one sounds livable." His grin disarmed her. "To tell the truth, I'd settle for a hard mattress anywhere. Atmosphere never did affect my sleep."

It affected Maggie's. An hour later she was dressed in a flannel nightgown and wrapped in the sleeping bag up to her chin. Mike had given her more than a reasonable time to be modestly cleared out of the bathroom and sound asleep before he came up. The door down the hall had closed a long time ago. She still wasn't tired. She clearly wasn't going to sleep.

Since she knew he'd chosen the green room, she had a dozen other choices of rooms to sleep in. On a whim, she'd opted for the madam's room. A disastrous mistake.

The blizzard was over outside. Moonlight poured in the windows, illuminating the blue silk draperies that hung around the bed, the mirrored wall and loveseat. The whole problem with the room, Maggie was discovering, was that it was lonely. It was a room for two, not one.

The draperies around the bed should have been closed, with a man and woman hidden behind them. Half filled glasses of champagne belonged on the exquisite little table, and clothes should have been strewn everywhere...a dangle of pearls here, a man's tuxedo cumberbund there. If she wanted to stretch her imagination a little further, she could conjure up the come-hither scent of a woman's long ago sultry perfume.

Unfortunately, she didn't need any more imagination. The man in the fantasy had Mike's eyes, Mike's hands, Mike's wickedly lazy smile. When she closed her eyes, he wasn't alone in a bed a long way down the hall. He was naked, in hers.

The problem was that the entire house was made for naughty fantasies. The spirit of the forbidden was part of the air. Everything about the house, the room, the man touched off long dormant yearnings in Maggie. The women in this house hadn't been inhibited the way she was. They'd reached out, taken risks, lived for the senses, completely unlike her.

When her daydreams refused to stop coming, Maggie tried to rationalize. Maybe this was natural? Didn't every decent woman have a secret wish to be sinful once in a lifetime? There was still no excuse for letting her imagination run away with her...particularly when it decided to dream up the soft flutter of wings near the ceiling. Her eyes blinked open in the darkness for the hundredth time. There was nothing there. She was going nuts, that was all.

Patience was called for. She forced her eyes closed again.

Something silky smooth touched her cheek. She ignored it, but the strange whirring noise persisted, faint, disturbing. She counted sheep. They all had brooding dark eyes. She switched to camels, and was distracted from that by the oddest smell.... Her eyes opened sleepily in the darkness—on two black spots. Two black eyes. Real eyes. Alive eyes.

"Holy Saint Patrick!" She unzipped her sleeping bag in three seconds flat, and still managed to trip on it on the way out the door. Grabbing the thing, she threw it over her head and stumbled into the hall. "Mike! *Michael!*"

The hall was dark; she couldn't remember which room was the green one... except that it had to be the only one with a closed door. It wasn't closed for long. Helter skelter she located the masculine bulk in the shadows and leaped for him. "Ianelli! For God's sake, there's something alive!"

"What the..."

"Oh, my God, I didn't close the door. It could get in here!"

She leaped off the bed again, slammed the bedroom door, then the closet door, then barreled onto the mattress again. Two firm strong hands reached for her shoulders, which didn't appreciably affect her momentum. It wasn't personal and it certainly wasn't sexual, but she had every intention of getting close. Preferably under-him close. Women's lib belonged in other mediums. He was bigger than she was, a fact of life she was more than willing to applaud.

"Maggie, what the hell are you—"

"I'm telling you it's real! It's got two beady eyes and it flies and it attacked me. You've got to believe me—"

"I believe you. I believe you. Calm down." Mike never woke from a sound sleep easily, nor was it simple trying to unwrap himself from the feminine ball Maggie was trying to make of herself. Her knee was in a dangerous place. One false move and he might never again be able to make love to a woman. And in the meantime she was trying to smother them both with her sleeping bag. She wanted to protect him, he realized belatedly.

First things first, he slid a hand down to readjust her knee. Second, he managed to grab the sleeping bag from her hands and give it a good fling. Then he groggily tried to get a look at her, but that wasn't so easy. It was pitch dark and Maggie was still trying to burrow—where, he wasn't sure. In time—it took him a moment—he did the obvious. Wrapped her up, tucked his chin to the crown of her head, and held her. "Flannery," he said soothingly, "it was probably a mouse."

"Mice don't fly."

He yawned. "A squirrel then. I'll take care of it. Relax. Relax, Maggie, nothing's going to happen. Nothing's going to hurt you." He added, very carefully, "Now you're sure you didn't imagine this."

Her head whipped up. "Look, I'm not an escapee from a mental ward. I'm telling you—"

"All right. All right. Just asking." He was still trying to clear the sleep from his eyes.

"It was real." And Mike was real. Real, warm and male, Maggie was suddenly realizing. About the same instant she stopped shaking, she considered starting again. From feel, she discovered he'd worn a T-shirt and jockey shorts to sleep in. His legs were strong, long, and blanketed with wiry hairs. His chest was solid and warm and he smelled good. She had to be imagining his smooth warm lips on her forehead.

"Okay now? No more trembling?"

"I . . . yes."

"Then, Maggie?"

"Hmmm?"

"Let go? So I can go take care of your monster?"

She unplastered herself from him with embarrassing speed. Mike climbed over her and groped for his jeans. Her eyes had long since adjusted to the darkness, and the room was silvery gray from the reflection of moonlight on snow. She could see his dark tousled head clearly, the way he unselfconsciously tugged on his jeans and zipped the zipper, then reached for his boots.

She couldn't imagine a more intimate act in a thousand years than watching a man zip up his pants. "I don't think you should go out there," she whispered.

"I've had lots of experience with monsters. Not to worry." Mike yawned again.

"Try to believe me, would you?"

"I do, I do."

"What if it bites you?"

"I'll bite back." Dressed—or at least as dressed as he was going to get—he leaned over to give her a swift, silencing kiss on the lips. "Would you relax? I realize that at the very least you think we've got a dragon out there, but believe me, I can handle it."

And then he was gone, the door carefully and quietly closed behind him. She could still feel the imprint, the taste of him, the smell and texture of Mike on her mouth. He had kissed her. There was no way on earth she could have fantasized that.

Three

———

Mike stumbled groggily through the dark hall with his senses still on half power. Alertness didn't begin to kick in until he paused in Maggie's bedroom doorway. Then the vague feral smell of a wild creature was unmistakable. The room was ominously and totally still . . . until he switched on the light.

Instantly a black winged shape zoomed for his face, protesting the light with a thin, high-pitched screech. As fast as he snapped off the overhead and jerked the door closed, Maggie cannoned into him from behind.

"What *is* it?"

"I thought you were safe and sound in my room," he said irritably. Instead she was standing barefooted in the freezing dark hallway. She had no robe over the white flannel nightgown and he couldn't imagine why she was carrying a towel.

"I want to apologize for acting like such an idiot. We can both handle whatever it is. I admit, I was shook up for a few minutes—"

"You were shaking like an earthquake." He observed, "You still are."

"I'm going to help."

Mike was tired. Trembling Irish-stubborn sprites weren't helping. "Maggie, I don't mind tackling this, really. I can do it better alone. Just go back to the room and—"

"Was it a squirrel?"

"No. I'm not positive what it is, but I'm reasonably sure..."

"What?" she said impatiently.

"A bat."

Her stomach sank. She had visions of some nice little captive squirrel or some strange breed of flying mouse. Bugs and spiders didn't bother her. Bats...bats were the pits. She opened her mouth and closed it again.

"I can handle it," Mike assured her. Damned if he couldn't feel a grin forming. What did she think she was going to take on with the towel for a weapon? "Just go back to the room," he coaxed.

She considered that, and then clamped chattering teeth together. "I'll go find you something you can...use." He was still arguing when she ran down the stairs.

Weapons didn't miraculously appear in an all-but-empty deserted house. The cupboards in the kitchen yielded a few old rags. Finally, she discovered a worn-out old broom in the back of the pantry and carried both it and the rags upstairs with her again.

"Terrific," Mike said with approval, and then more firmly, "Okay. You've done your share. Now let me handle it from here, all right?"

She started to protest, but he hardly left her much choice when he promptly closed himself inside the madam's room.

He switched on the light again and his lips compressed at the creature's abrasive scream. The damn thing looked four feet long as it winged its way from corner to corner. He swung the broom once, missed, then aimed a second time and missed again.

The third time he hit the creature. Folded up, the fruit bat was only a bit of a thing. He wrapped it in the rags, pushed open the bedroom door again and made for the stairs and front door.

Once the creature had been disposed of, he returned inside and paced for several minutes in front of the glowing embers of the fire. Chances were good that the thing had nested in a chimney and gotten in through an open flue. Obviously, it couldn't have entered where he'd set the fire, which left the second downstairs fireplace. He checked that flue with the flame of a match, but the damper stuck and he still wasn't satisfied. A closet finally yielded an old dusty fireplace screen, which he used to block the hearth opening. After a brisk wash of his hands he wearily mounted the stairs.

The last thing he expected to see was Maggie still standing there waiting for him. Her arms were wrapped around herself, she was clearly freezing, and she looked tired enough to fall asleep standing up. She must have run her hands through her hair a dozen times because it looked like tangled silk. "You're trying to get pneumonia?" he suggested.

"I should have helped you. I can't stand women who pull a screaming meemy routine."

"Bats are acceptable screaming meemy material," he said gently. Abruptly, he added, "Thanks. For waiting." He couldn't think of the last time anyone had waited for him for anything. Just as abruptly, he said, "Anyway, there's nothing to worry about. The fireplace's closed and there's no way another creature could get in."

He waited. She didn't move toward her room.

"Maggie? Everything's all right now," he repeated.

"Yes, I heard you."

"There's nothing else in your room. I promise you."

"Yes."

He waited. A light was on in the green room at the far end of the hall. In the semi-darkness where they were standing, he could see the luster of her hair and her pale soft skin but not her eyes. They were pinned on the door to the madam's room. "Why am I getting the feeling," he said slowly, "that you're not going back in there?"

"Oh, I will. In time. You go on ahead to sleep. I'll be fine here." She smiled at him, brilliantly. "Mice are okay. Bats just aren't my thing. In time..."

In time? From the way her feet were rooted to the floor, he gathered she intended to move by 1990. For a moment Mike was completely motionless. Then he yawned, rubbed the back of his neck, and shook his head. "Flannery?" He said tactfully, "Are we talking about putting the two sleeping bags together?"

"Well..."

"Come on." His tone held exasperation, humor, exhaustion, gentleness. He didn't know where the gentleness came from. He didn't consider himself a gentle man.

"I'm sorry—"

"Don't be silly. I'm scared witless of the damn things myself." He switched on the overhead in his room. "It's colder in here than in your room—either way's all right by me, but it'll probably make the more comfortable bed if we zip the sleeping bags together."

"Much warmer," she concurred, and as fast as he finished zipping, she crawled into the far side of the sleeping bag. The room was pitch black when he snapped off the light. She could only hear him quietly shucking his jeans. "Sleep feet out or feet in?" he demanded.

"In."

"Face left or right?"

"It doesn't matter."

"Good, because I always have to sleep facing the door. Unbreakable habit," he admitted, in a casual tone that reeked of don't-worry-I-can't-tell-you-how-safe-you-are. "Keep in mind that if you're a tosser and turner, I'll probably beat you."

Since he meant her to smile, she did, just before he crawled into his side of the sleeping bag. Zipped together, the bags held ample room for lovers, but not necessarily for two people who simply needed or chose to sleep together.

"Turn the other way," Mike told her.

She faced the window as he dropped down beside her and carefully turned his back to her. She doubted he'd given himself any more than breathing space but actually felt physical contact with him in only three spots: her right shoulder blade, her right lower back, and approximately a quarter inch dot on her fanny. All three spots developed a heartbeat all their own.

"You'll sleep now?" Mike murmured.

"Yes."

"No more worrying, Maggie."

"No more worrying," she agreed.

She thought about that for a long time. Minutes ticked by, and then more than minutes. She thought about worrying, and she thought about fear of bats, and she thought about a man who assumed he had to handle every problem alone. She thought about the madam's room, and about fantasies, and about the kind of woman she wasn't.

And when she heard his exhausted sigh, she quietly, slowly—like someone else was doing it—turned.

Her arm slid around his waist and her breasts nuzzled into his back. And then she laid, very still.

"Flannery?"

"Hmmm."

"Turn around." His voice was flat, suddenly not so sleepy.

She hesitated. "I don't think so."

Silence invaded the dark room, along with naughty fantasies, wild dreams, and sleepy possibilities. The house was haunted with the spirit of bold, brazen women who took their own sexuality for granted... not with women like Maggie, who was suddenly trembling to beat the band.

Mike moved with infinite slowness, turning without promoting any more touch than was necessary to face her, not an easy task to accomplish in the confines of the double sleeping bag. He did touch her then. His hand reached out in the darkness to find her cheek. One of his fingers gently traced the line of her cheekbone. "No," he said softly. "You're tired and you were scared, Margaret Mary Flannery. You're not thinking straight. Now..."

Someone reached up to shut him up, with soft lips cradling over his. It certainly wasn't a girl raised to be a saint. It certainly wasn't Margaret Mary, who'd barely had the sexual experience to fit in a tea cup, much less any experience in seducing a man. It also wasn't a woman who'd never had a one-night stand in her life and certainly didn't want one now.

But there would never be another time, another Mike, another man she wanted this much, or another lonely night exactly like this one. She doubted she'd have another chance to conceivably be a different woman than she really was, or to reach out to a man in the way she'd always wanted to.

Maggie really had no excuses. A little voice in her head was scolding about immorality. Her heart was ticking guilt, and her lips wooed his with soft, beguiling, "take me" kisses. Her fingers stole up to touch his cheek, then sneaked in his hair to mold him closer. Her body turned as pliant as a willow in the wind. The tips of her breasts wantonly brushed his chest; her slim leg slid between his muscular ones.

"Maggie."

She'd burn for this. Of that she had no doubts.

"Maggie..."

She was terrified he might be immune to all this. He wasn't. At first, his lips lay absolutely still against hers and his body turned rigid. That wasn't the same thing as totally rejecting her however, and gradually like the helpless way sleep overcame a tired man, she felt his tension lessen.

His mouth suddenly shared in the kiss. His tongue intruded inside her mouth, delving into sweetness, seduced into taking honey, wanting honey, needing it.

Her head was suddenly pressed into the down mattress, and her shy wooing kiss took on hunger. His. In one long sweep his hand smoothed up and down her spine, ingraining the fabric of nightgown to her skin. His splayed hand urged her bottom tight against him.

Liquid gold flowed through her veins, a sensation she'd never imagined before. The touch of Mike was right, as was the smell and feel of him, the warmth of him. The yearning had been inside of her for forever, waiting for him.

Abruptly his hand lifted to her face and pushed back her hair. Dark brooding eyes seared on hers in the darkness. "Honey, no. You don't know what you're doing. This isn't what you want."

Those brooding eyes demanded honesty. She gave it to him, her voice halting and low. "There was one man. A few years ago, and a painful disaster. He respected me. Too much. I think he had very definite ideas about how a 'good woman' was supposed to respond—or not respond. Don't respect me, would you, Mike?" She whispered desperately, "Can't I just give you a gift? For free, Ianelli, no strings. It's a dark, cold, lonely night. Am I really the only one who's lonely?"

"Maggie...." He felt a rare surge of helplessness. He'd never taken advantage of a woman in his life, and to make love with Maggie was unquestionably to take advantage of her. He knew damn well she'd have a hard time living with a one-night fling. She'd all but told him she'd never been around.

Except that pictures of her "one man" roused a core of something in Mike that he hadn't felt in a long time. Only a fool and a bastard would have made love to Maggie and left her feeling less of a woman.

She was a very real woman. She was also so close. She smelled like violets and her skin had the softness of untouched dew. He ached with loneliness and she was there. Willing. Don't you touch her, Ianelli. Don't you dare lay a finger on her. Another man will teach her about love. She'll find the right man, and it sure isn't you. You're broke and out of a job and don't have a damn thing to offer her.

Except for the one thing she seemed to want. And except that he abruptly discovered he didn't want another man to teach her about love.

"Listen," he said gruffly, "if I thought for one minute you wouldn't regret this in the morning—"

"I won't."

"You will, Maggie."

"I won't."

He leaned over her. She could see the frown wedged on his forehead. She could see his jaw working to say something else and she could feel his fingers, sifting softly through her hair. His eyes finally shifted to hers. What she saw there chilled her blood, then heated it so fast her heart stopped beating.

Eyes locked, his palm impossibly gentle on the side of her face, he said softly, "You know I'd never hurt you?"

She nodded, but didn't know that at all. At that instant, she was certain that Mike had the incredible power to hurt her as no man ever had, that he was going to do it and she was going to let him. The risk was nothing important, not once his hands framed her face and he christened her lips with a kiss so gentle she forgot to think.

He tucked her half-beneath him, so she could feel his weight, become used to the feel of his muscled legs and hard chest, and learn all the smells and textures and tastes that were Mike. His lips traced her lips in slow lazy kisses that nuzzled and teased and then claimed her soft mouth.

Like a dove let free to soar, she felt inhibitions flee, her senses burst to life. His skin was sleek and smooth under the T-shirt. His hair felt like a mink's fur under her fingers, thick and luxurious. His mouth moved to her throat. Her heartbeat moved there. His hands roamed down to the curve of her waist. Her heartbeat moved there. The throb and pulse kept shifting, growing louder, stronger, more intense.

The room was so dark and cold everywhere that Mike wasn't. "Just this once" roared in her ears, blocking out sense and reason. There would only be this once. Exactly what should have made it wrong made it right. She touched as she'd always wanted to touch a man. Her lover in the darkness wouldn't settle for less.

"Lift, little one." Mike's voice was throaty, low.

She was cold for a second when he tugged off her nightgown. For the shortest moment moonlight brushed her small breasts and body with silver. For the longest moment she felt Mike's intimate gaze, and then his eyes traveled up to hers, dark, luminous in passion, male and primitive in intent. She suddenly felt as vulnerable as a butterfly caught in the wind.

The feeling didn't lessen when he stopped long enough to tug off first his T-shirt, then the last of his underwear. He never stopped looking at her because he couldn't.

He'd expected a lady who needed infinite gentleness and patience. He'd expected to feel the basic sexual response any man felt for an attractive woman when he'd been deprived of intimacy for a long time. He hadn't anticipated how sweetly she gave, how deliciously she reacted to her own sensuality, how vibrantly she responded in passion.

When he slid back down beside her, she wrapped around him, breasts, tummy, thighs molded to his. Willingly she matched him caress for caress, yet she stayed pressed like silky iron when his hand tried to roam between their bodies. Her mouth absorbed his tongue; her hands absorbed his texture. She was busy, so busy. He made a sound when her lips tasted his collarbone. He shuddered when her fingertips wandered down to his hips. There was so much she wanted to know, needed to learn, craved to feel. Yet at another level, she felt his hand at the side of her breast, and she locked closer again.

His lips suddenly touched hers in a different way. The kiss was light, gentle, soothing. "No," he scolded softly. "Let me."

"I just..."

"You're built slight; is that why you're suddenly turning shy on me?" His mouth hovered over hers; his hand smoothed back her hair. "Ah, Maggie, you should never have shown me where you were vulnerable."

He shifted her hands out of the way, and scolded her shyness with kisses that started at her throat and moved down with infinite slowness. He found exactly what he wanted. She shivered suddenly, inside and out. It wasn't that she was so foolish about her small breasts; it was just that she wanted to be perfect for him.

His tongue swirled lazy, slow circles around first her right nipple, then her left. His lips traced the soft undersides of her breasts. His palm kneaded and stroked and cupped. He pressed his night beard in the tender valley between sensitive flesh, then let his smooth warm lips apologize for that roughness. When he was finished she had no doubt of any kind what he felt about perfect and Maggie and breasts. When he was finished, her hands were trying to clutch at him, force his mouth back to hers, demand that he come to her.

"Are we ever going to make that mistake again, little one?" he whispered.

"No. Mike . . . please."

His mouth was suddenly everywhere, on her temple, her nose, her chin, her lips. She couldn't talk. The room was dark, but she could see Mike's face, the grave intentness his features took on in passion, the relentless black fire in his eyes that was trying to swallow her up, devour her. "Yes," he murmured. "That's exactly how it's going to be. Like a slow steady burn. Like fire. Lord, you're beautiful . . ."

She wasn't. It was him. He didn't understand at all that she wasn't Maggie this night, but someone else, another woman, a wildly sensual woman. It had to do with Mike and the man he was, not her.

And the woman he'd made reached out, enclosed him in softness, protected him from loneliness and darkness and cold with a fierceness she didn't begin to understand. A shallow cry escaped her lips when he filled her, then another cry and another. In giving, she took. In yielding, she claimed. The starburst of pleasure was for both of them.

Maggie woke in an absolutely freezing room to the gray glare of morning light. She sensed Mike was gone even before she noticed that his clothes had disappeared. No sound from downstairs disturbed the silence; she guessed intuitively that there was no one in the house with her.

Guilt hit her with all the subtlety of a tidal wave. Four thousand Hail Marys aren't going to get you out of this one, Margaret Mary. What have you done?

Thrown herself at the poor man, that's what she'd done. Her first penance was flinging off the sleeping bag and feeling ice cold air rush over her bare skin. Following that, she liberally punished her face with splashes of cold water in the bathroom, followed by brushing her teeth until her gums ached and attacking her hair with a brush until it crackled. Such small penances didn't do a thing for guilt, and the face staring back at her in the old wavery mirror still looked unfailingly wholesome, healthy, and glowing. Extra glowing, actually.

And her bright complexion was accented by a helpless smile and a vulnerable sparkle in her green eyes. Did she dare tell him how special the night had been, that she'd never dreamed she was capable of that kind of sensuality? Because of him she felt stronger as a woman, more open to a world of choices, richer, sexier, more alive.

Of course you can't tell him that, she scolded herself as she searched through the madam's room for her clothes. She tugged on jeans and thick socks, then yanked on a bulky red sweater that stretched over her hips. What you're going to do, she told herself, is start behaving like a nice, decent woman. You're going to somehow make him understand that he's safe from the clutches of latent nymphomaniacs and that you're not going to throw yourself at him again. Dammit, he'd made it clear as glass that he wasn't interested from the minute they'd met.

Downstairs, she found a fire blazing, a cracked kettle simmering coffee on the hearth, and a note on the couch. He'd gone to check the condition of the roads, pick up food, and call the caretaker. Did he also want to escape from a woman who embarrassed him?

The guilt was deserved, but it certainly wasn't helping her feel purged in any way. She had to get her mind off Mike. Foraging in her duffel bag, she came up with a banana and a box of raisins and wandered to the window. The blizzard might never have happened. A shamelessly bright winter sun reigned over a landscape dipped in crystals. Icicles dripped from the eaves; rivulets of water ran down dark tree trunks like long diamonds.

The night before she hadn't realized how much of the house was actually built over the river. Today the banks looked swollen; water bridged the ice-encrusted shore and twisted in long snakes through the snow.

Wooden posts jutted out from the water; she guessed they were used as boat moorings in the past, but now they were barely visible. Was the river always this high, or was it just because of this time of year?

Did she care? Dragging a hand through her hair, she tried to concentrate on exploring the house. She wandered, touching the newel posts of the mahogany banister, the brass light fixtures, the cool marble of the hearth. The mahogany paneling on the inside wall beneath the stairs was exquisite. She touched the wood grain and then paused, frowning.

The paneling was uneven in spots. Seams didn't match. Her fingers discovered an odd gnarl in the wood . . . and to her shock, the wall gave beneath her fingertips. She nearly fell over when an invisible door sprang open. Inside was a dark cubicle the size of a walk-in closet, shaped to match the triangle made by the stairwell.

She ducked and took a step in—then out again. "Bats" flashed through her mind. She reached more cautiously for a light switch, but there wasn't one. Still, her eyes lit on the shadowed shape of three steamer trunks.

Bats couldn't possibly have gotten in here, she assured herself . . . or else she'd just have to face them, because there was no way on earth she could just stand there and ignore the trunks. Gingerly edging forward, she reached for the top one and started tugging. It couldn't be empty. *Nothing* that heavy could be empty.

Blowing a wisp of hair from her cheeks, she tugged and pulled until the first trunk finally crashed toward her. She dragged it a few feet into daylight and started fumbling with the latches. The brass and leather wrappings were old and stuck shut, but it wasn't locked. Gramps's treasure, she thought fleetingly. She lost two nails trying to open the darn thing, and didn't care. For the first time that morning, she started laughing.

Four

***

Mike set a grocery bag down on the porch steps, and tromped through the ice and snow to the river's edge at the back of the house. Through narrowed eyes he viewed the rising water, then the bright sun, then the innocuous-looking gray band of clouds in the west.

The caretaker claimed the river "only took it in its mind to flood every fifty years or so." The locals claimed this was the year. Talk in the country store where Mike had bought the groceries was all speculation on "when," not "if." Blizzard-thaw conditions had plagued Indiana for the last two months. Another eight inches of snow had fallen the night before, yet today the sun was beaming down with an intensity that was all but springlike.

The concrete foundation of the house was built to take a flooding. In fact, Whistler had told him the main entrance of the place used to be right on the water. Customers parked their boats beneath and took the steps up into the lodge—a discreet way for a staunch Republican to get a glass of wine during prohibition times, no doubt.

This was fine, but if the river flooded he and Maggie had no way to get out.

With a last frown at the clouds in the west, Mike slugged his hands in his pockets and stalked back toward the front door. It was only ten in the morning, but he'd been up for hours. He hadn't slept well in months. Sometimes he dreamed he proved himself clear of accusations against him and sometimes his dreams were full of anger and frustration. They were always nightmares of a kind. A man needed work.

Usually, he woke in a cold sweat. This morning he'd risen to a soft body sprawled all over him and a fan of dark copper hair on his face. His step suddenly quickened. He grabbed the brown sack and pushed open the door.

"You're back!" Maggie's flushed face met him.

"I thought you still might be sleeping." Her bulky red sweater hid any trace of a figure; there was a streak of dirt on her cheek a mile wide; and no one had brighter eyes than Maggie's. Mike stashed the grocery bag in the corner of the couch, then shed his jacket. "What have you gotten into?"

"Treasures." She motioned.

He could see the trunk. And clothes...a woman's white satin dress, a short thing completely done up with fringe—most of it straggly. Some kind of long scarf, moth-eaten. A wrinkled gown in emerald satin, a man's tuxedo. He glanced, then snatched a styrofoam cup from the grocery sack and headed for the coffee pot on the hearth. "Why on earth would anyone have saved such junk? Where'd you find it?"

"Junk!"

Mike cleared his throat. "Real finds?" He tried to put more enthusiasm in his voice.

"I found them through a secret passage. Watch this." She demonstrated how the hidden door opened in the paneling.

"Ah, more intrigue and mysteries," Mike said dryly. "Maybe we both should have expected that sort of thing—anything's possible in a house built to hide things from the law." He paused en route to filling his cup with coffee. He could hardly have missed the quick flush that colored Maggie's cheeks when he had first walked in. And he didn't miss now how rapidly she turned away from him.

Maggie bent down and started folding things back in the trunk. She could feel his gaze on her hair. Her hand whipped back to straighten it. She could feel his eyes on her shoulders. She instantly forced them to relax. All she could think of was making sure he knew he didn't have to worry about her coming on to him again.

"Well," she said briskly, "I'll just sort through the rest of this and get it out of the way. You must be starving. I brought things we could have for breakfast . . . lunch, too.''

"More goodies from that duffel bag of yours?" he asked lightly. "I think you packed enough to survive a war, little one."

The 'little one' flowed in and out of her veins like heated honey. Don't do that to me, Mike. Don't pretend you feel something you don't. "I did," she admitted wryly. She was so busy folding that she didn't have to look at him. "On the other hand, you're likely to get pretty tired of peanut butter and dried fruits by dinner time—"

"I brought steaks for dinner. They'll keep cold enough outside until we're ready to broil them—and I brought other food, Maggie. I hardly expected you to feed either one of us." He hesitated. If she folded the green dress any more times, it was likely to become a ball. "Sleep all right?" he asked casually.

"Just fine. Terrific, in fact."

"I talked to the real estate man from the pay phone at the store. He promised to see the place next week—"

"About listing it, you mean?"

"About listing it to sell it," he agreed, and watched the slight straightening of her spine with a feeling of wariness. "Maggie—"

"I went to a seminar last fall."

"Did you?"

"A boring thing, on women in management. The woman who gave it was good, though. Her name was Dorothy Langley."

"How nice," Mike murmured.

"Dorothy gives twelve seminars a year. All at motels. She absolutely hates them—motels, that is." Maggie knew better than to present a half-baked idea that she'd only thought about for an hour, but she decided that anything was better than a private, personal conversation with Mike. "She says that companies these days want more for their employees than the knowledge that goes into a seminar. They're smart enough to know that their executives and managers need a chance to relax, wind down. Not only because they absorb the information better in a relaxed atmosphere, but because they come back to work with more motivation and purpose—"

"Maggie, I can't tell you how fascinating this conversation is, but—"

"This place, you know, would be perfect. Like an executive retreat? Dorothy gives seminars on marketing, women in management and financial management. There have to be dozens of people like her, who give banking seminars or motivation seminars or strategy-planning seminars. All of them need a place . . . and this place has everything. Space, and a quiet atmosphere, a *personal* atmosphere. The kitchen's huge. All those acres to walk and relax in, the river—we could have boats. There were boats here before, weren't there? We'd have to close off a few rooms downstairs, but not all of it . . ."

Unfortunately out of breath, Maggie risked a quick glance at Mike, and just as quickly turned away. Maybe he'd heard the idea and maybe he hadn't. His eyes were fixed on hers, and his mouth was forming a determined line. He tossed the empty cup in his hand. "You *have* been busy thinking." He added deliberately, "And only about the house, right, Maggie?"

She knew he was coming up behind her, because she could feel the shiver that started at the base of her spine and her palms grew damp. She folded, fast. "I know that kind of thing would take an impossible amount of capital. But a few acres sold off might provide some of it. And banks...darn it, banks have nothing to do all day long but loan money—"

"Sssh, little one." Lord, she was stiff. He touched her shoulders, gently turned her to face him, and simply wrapped up one rigid Maggie. The top of her head nestled exactly right under his chin. She was trembling.

She was also babbling. "You don't have to be involved if you don't want to, Ianelli. I already know you want to sell it—"

"I'd be happy—particularly at the moment—if the entire property dropped in the river."

"And obviously I couldn't immediately buy you out, but once I got the thing going, I could make payments. If you're afraid I don't have the background to make a go of the thing...I think I do. All I've ever worked in was manufacturing, but managing a product involves sales, advertising, production, marketing. It isn't so dissimilar—"

"Maggie, would you cut it out? We can argue inheritances another time." Her hair was such a mess. His fingers slowly finger-brushed it, soothing her, quieting her. "It was a good night," he said slowly. "One I have no intention of forgetting. There's nothing to run from, nothing to be embarrassed about. You think I don't understand what happened?"

"Mike—"

"It's called a cold dark night, strangers, loneliness, and a house that's made up of fantasy material. You got caught up in wanting to be someone else for a few short hours. You think you're the only one that's ever happened to?" He tilted her chin so he could see her eyes. "It was a night you needed to reach out to someone. I'm just glad it was me," he said quietly, fiercely.

She didn't know what to do but look at him. He was exactly right but so terribly wrong. Yes, it had been a night when she needed to reach out, but she had a lifetime of inhibitions behind her that told her she'd never have reached out to just any stranger. She'd reacted to Mike from the minute she'd met him as she'd never reacted to another man.

"Maggie, I value nothing on earth as much as honesty," he said gently. "You came to me with honesty last night and I hope you know you never have to lie or pretend with me about anything. I would never think the less of you for having needs. I *would* think the less of you if you'd invented some kind of nonsense about love. You don't love me—you don't even know me. We shared something far more real than that, something far more valuable. And you don't have to be afraid I'm going to pursue it. I knew last night that was a one time thing for you."

Her eyes searched his. There was the oddest lump in her throat. In his own way, he was telling her he didn't believe in love, or at least that he believed in honesty more. Honesty for Maggie was that she'd fallen painfully in love with him approximately three and a half seconds after she'd met him. Honesty for Maggie was that she wanted him to pursue it.

And honesty was knowing he didn't want to hear any of that.

"Friends?" He touched her cheek.

"Friends." She managed a smile.

He grinned then, stepped back, and dropped his hands loosely onto his hips. "All right then. Now why do I have the feeling you're going to want to spend the rest of the day searching for more secret passage-ways?"

Mike gave a worried look at the late afternoon sky. The temperature was well above freezing, and the sun had long since disappeared behind clouds. No rain or snow was forecast, but he'd feel better altogether when the cold night rolled in and ended the thawing conditions.

Propelled by a brilliant throwing arm, a snowball lobbed high came close to colliding with a tree branch, missed, soared free and then promptly plummeted. A white splat landed flat between Mike's eighth and ninth vertebrae.

Maggie rubbed her gloved hands together in the traditional gesture of a job well done. She stopped rubbing abruptly when Mike turned, hands on hips and dark eyes glowering.

"What was that for?"

She mimicked his stance, hands on hips, legs spread wide. "I thought we were taking this walk to relax, Ianelli. You have this big problem with relaxing."

"So you thought shooting me with a snowball would help?"

She shook her head, and moved ahead of him toward the house. "I think you're hopeless."

"Thanks." Mike smiled, then quietly, smoothly bent down to gather a moundful of snow. He packed it expertly, making a perfect ball. Maggie was three steps ahead of him, then four. Her jacket was waist length. Beneath that, her jeans molded precisely to a small, perfectly formed fanny. His eyes narrowed, anticipating his target.

She'd reached the porch steps when the snowball was launched. Her hand was on the doorknob when her hips did a sudden bump and grind reminiscent of a disco dancer. During the 'bump' the snowball splatted flat against the door molding. Maggie was inside and looking out within seconds. "Never mind," she called back consolingly. "We all have these failures, Ianelli. Very few have ever bested a Flannery, if that makes you feel any better."

"Come back here and say that a little closer. I couldn't hear you."

She shook her head, laughing. "My stomach is grumbling for those steaks you bought. If I don't eat soon, I'm going to collapse."

Unlikely, Mike thought dryly. The woman had more energy than a construction gang promised overtime. She refueled on life, not food.

Inside, he stomped the snow from his boots and tugged off his jacket, noting without surprise that Maggie's hat had dropped to the floor, her gloves were already on the mantle and her jacket had been tossed near the door. Maggie never stopped moving long enough to be either tidy or organized.

They'd discovered two more of her hidden passageways during the day. One was inside a closet in one of the upstairs bedrooms. The other was a small anteroom off the pantry that opened to a spring catch. Inside was a stool, a rickety lamp, and assorted fifty-year-old canned goods that had tickled Maggie. They'd explored the lower level, where customers at another time might have parked their boats, paused at the wine cellar, and entered the lodge through a "floor door" that looked like an escape hatch. They'd discovered a loose floorboard in the madam's room, that opened to reveal a copper lined storage compartment clearly designed to hide something—liquor, Mike had told Maggie.

They'd checked out the fuses and the electrical system, the plumbing and furnace. Maggie had opened every cupboard and drawer, found some old newspapers she used to clean windows with, and had whipped a rag and broom around until the place almost looked clean.

She showed no signs of wearing out. Mike had suggested the walk to slow both of them down and then

watched Maggie prance off in the snow like she was
ready for a twenty-mile hike. Now she was still on the
move. Fanny in the air, she was rummaging in her
duffel bag and surfaced, grinning like she'd found
diamonds, with salt and pepper for their steaks.

He was not surprised any longer by anything that
came out of her duffel bag. He was no longer surprised by anything Maggie did. For the first time in
months, he'd spent a day not haunted by his worry
about work. Mike kept telling himself that her un-
flagging enthusiasm was annoying, that her optimism
was naive.

Only he'd never come across a life celebrator quite
like Maggie. The woman could package sunshine and
his life had been gray for months.

He rolled up his shirtsleeves, paced toward the fire.
"I suppose I'm expected to cook this dinner?"

"You certainly aren't. I've never cooked over a fire,
and I'm a big believer in trying anything once. What
you can do is sit with your feet propped up and enjoy
the hors d'oeuvres."

Hors d'oeuvres were a mix of peanuts and raisins,
served in a styrofoam cup.

"Eat hearty," Maggie encouraged him. "Heaven
knows I'll burn the steaks."

She did. They were charred on the outside and
blood red within when she served them on paper
plates. Cooked on the embers, the baked potatoes
were a little raw, and they had no butter. Dessert was
butterscotch candies—every pocket she had seemed to

produce a butterscotch disc. They were clearly Maggie's vice.

"This is conceivably the best meal I've ever had," Mike pronounced. It bothered him no end that he meant it.

Sacked on the opposite couch with an arm curved behind her for a pillow, Maggie said from behind closed eyes, "The only trick to getting compliments as a cook is making sure the man is darned close to starvation before you feed him." She opened one eye long enough to accurately aim her stockinged foot at Mike's calf. "The dishes are on you, Ianelli."

"That amounts to little more than silverware. Are you sure you think I can handle it?"

"After that you can make some fresh coffee," she said firmly. "If I don't get something soon to revive me, I'm afraid it's curtains."

"Don't tell me the lady is finally running out of steam?"

Maggie wasn't even close to running out of energy, but she didn't tell Mike that. She also didn't mention that she wasn't at all the Pollyanna that Mike seemed determined to think she was.

Maybe she did tend toward optimism. Maybe the house had sparked every impulsive, imaginative streak she'd ever had, but Maggie was no fool. Mike had done something very special for her the night before. She'd found a gift to give him back over the long hours of the day.

Laughter. Whatever had put the brooding in his dark eyes, whatever made him avoid answering the most casual personal question, whatever was haunting one Michael Ianelli was probably none of her business, but when Maggie took up a cause, it was generally with bulldog stubbornness. Mike may not want a less-than-buxom, green-eyed lover, but he was stuck with a woman determined to chase the brooding away.

In the kitchen, she heard the sound of silverware clinking under a stream of water and surged to her feet. When Mike returned, she was ready for him. Gramps's trunks had yielded riches.

Standing behind one of the casino tables, she had two cups of whiskey poured and waiting. A feather boa scarf was swathed around her neck over her red sweater. Her figure had miraculously changed shape. A fedora hat was perched on her head; a rhinestone cigarette holder was clamped between her lips; and she was shuffling a deck of cards.

Mike had only taken a step into the room when he halted. She batted her eyelashes at his startled expression. "Let's see the color of your money, darling. And let's hope you're prepared to lose *big* money, sweetheart. I *love* taking a handsome man's money."

Mike threw back his head and laughed. "What happened to the lady I left sacked out for an after-dinner nap on the couch?"

"I sent her home, the little mouse." She cocked her finger at him, and crooned seductively, "This is a private game. She couldn't possibly keep up with the action I intend to offer you, stranger."

"Oh?" Mike drew up the rusty stool she'd brought in from God only knew where, and folded his arms on the casino table. It was her own darn fault he couldn't keep his eyes from her breasts. "How well...endowed you are," he mentioned.

She gave him a profile shot. Her sudden bustiness looked suspiciously squared off at the edges and was slightly lop-sided. Noting that, she hefted the right side to match the left.

Mike put his head in his hands.

She stared at him, deliberately not smiling. "You think it's a little much, do you?" Maggie drawled.

"I think it's beyond belief."

"To tell the truth, this new figure of mine is a little uncomfortable." Her hand snuck beneath the sweater. She drew out first one roll of toilet paper, then a second. "I just happened to have them—"

"In your duffel bag, I know. You did pack for any possible problem, didn't you, Maggie?"

"You think you're so smart, Ianelli? Let's see the color of your money." When he reached into his back pocket for his wallet, her eyes widened in alarm. "Not paper money, you fool. Change. Pennies."

"Oh. A really big game."

"You got it, handsome." She started dealing. Her voice resumed its breathy huskiness. "Save your paper money for later." She motioned her head toward the stairs. "We've got any action your little heart could desire in this place. For a price, of course. Beautiful women," she batted her eyelashes again. "Whiskey, gambling—"

"Sass."

"Oh, hush." She picked up her cards. "Five card stud. Ladies wild."

"Believe me, I guessed that."

She couldn't play poker worth a damn. He forced her to switch to gin rummy, but then beat her at that, too. The fire crackled behind them. Night settled in the corners, and filled all the empty spaces. But the niche where they were remained bright.

Mike couldn't take his eyes off Maggie. The feathery boa scarf around her neck was straggly and motheaten and looked ridiculous over her sweater. The fedora was too big. After two small paper cups of whiskey she was edging toward tipsy. And her eyes were endless green.

She kept trying to sneak little hints into the conversation about keeping the house. And seeing all the potential that was there waiting for them to take advantage of it. All he could see was the potential that was in Maggie.

Outside, he was totally conscious that the wind had picked up, that another storm made staying in the house another night potentially dangerous. Inside there were other dangers, in a pixie with dark red hair and big green eyes who could almost make him believe in fantasies as much as she did.

"The hour's getting pretty late. Think it's about time to start folding up?" It was time to go to bed. To get away from her, before he did something he knew he'd regret.

"I hate sleeping," she mentioned illogically, and dealt another hand.

They played out two more before she called it quits. She should have known better than to drink alcohol; it inevitably made her sleepy. Mike disposed of the paper cups and took care of the fire while she stored her scarf, hat and toys back in the trunk.

They seemed to end up ready to climb the stairs at the same time. Maggie klutzily stumbled over the first one. Mike chuckled, and wrapping an arm around her shoulder, helped her conquer the rest of the stairs. "Drink a lot, do you?"

"Normally, I have the sense to stick to Perrier."

"The only thing you neglected to pack in that tote of yours."

"You should see me on a camping trip. I pack the house, garage and driveway."

"A little rough to carry, surely?"

"Never underestimate the power of a woman, Ianelli." She yawned when she reached the top of the stairs and smiled a simple, uncomplicated smile at him. She'd loved every moment of their evening and of the day. If she'd fallen in love with the man he didn't have to know it.

Expecting a return smile from Mike, she didn't get it. He didn't easily drop his hand from her shoulder either. Standing in the dim lit hall, his expression suddenly changed. His lazy easy humor disappeared. His eyes settled on hers, wouldn't let go. And his hand on her shoulder suddenly lifted to touch the strands of her hair around her cheek.

Her heart skipped a beat. Easy chatter had skimmed from her lips all night; suddenly her throat went dry. "Tired?" she said finally. "It's been a long day."

"Yes." Don't touch her. Leave her alone, Ianelli. She's had a little too much to drink, you haven't. But her auburn hair felt like silk in his fingers. The second floor was colder than the first, the shadows darker, the night lonelier.

"I suppose . . . we should go off to bed."

"Yes." There was nothing in hell he had to give her. He had no job, no security, and as far as he knew, no future. All day long he'd been careful to preserve that distance of strangers, to avoid any comments about his personal life.

Except that Maggie was a beautiful and sensually desirable woman. He badly wanted to be absolutely sure she knew that. He wasn't so egotistical to think that she'd ever wanted him, she didn't even know who Michael Ianelli was. Maggie had reached out to a stranger the night before because she'd needed a lover she didn't know. Perhaps she didn't really want to know or ever meet him again. She'd come to him with doubts about herself as a woman and with faith that his lovemaking would take them away. Her blind trust had been foolish, dangerous, and it had touched him. Being a fantasy lover was the only thing he could give Maggie.

His lips dipped down to brush hers. It could have ended with nothing more than that, a light kiss, a shared moment before sleep. Nothing more than affection had to be implicit in the pairing of two lips.

Except that her mouth suddenly trembled beneath his. Her fingers curled on the sleeve of his sweater. And those huge green eyes of hers turned into a woman's emerald fire, a shy spark ignited just that quickly.

Maggie couldn't breathe. He drew back from that first kiss and just looked at her. Heat rushed through her veins at the look. His lips drew up in the faintest smile before they came down again.

His body slid into hers; his arms slowly wrapped around her waist, stole behind her back. He tasted like whiskey, like butterscotch, like Mike. He tasted warm and hopelessly desirable. Her fingers climbed his sleeves to his shoulders and held on. He caressed her like a man who couldn't let go. He kissed her like she was infinitely beautiful, infinitely small, infinitely female. He kissed her like he could drain a woman of will with the simple act of touching tongues.

"Maggie..."

Whatever he was going to say was lost. His lips were suddenly skimming over her cheeks, her brow, her chin, back to her lips again. This time her head reeled back from the pressure of his mouth. Silky pressure. Hungry pressure. And when his head finally lifted again, his breathing was hoarse.

"Maggie..."

"Hmmm?"

"Are you," he murmured lowly, "going to make me sleep alone?"

Five

Maggie wanted to answer him, but for that minute couldn't. A dark dusty hall had just turned magical. In that dark hall, fantasies were suddenly real—a very strong man could suddenly admit to need; a plain woman could be fiercely desired; a good woman could become dangerously wanton.

Magic wasn't real, yet the man in front of her was. She tried to think, and couldn't. It was a very simple question he'd asked her, the same question men had been asking women since time began. There was nothing complicated. "No" was the wise answer. "Yes" the magical one.

She studied the uneven throb of his Adam's apple, his mouth, and murmured, "Do you think you could kiss me again?"

She hadn't realized how tense Mike was, until she felt the unsteadiness of his hands framing her face. Until her lips felt that first wisp of a kiss, so alluring and tender that she was forced to wind her arms around his neck.

"Ah, Maggie...."

His voice suddenly sounded thicker. Conversation began and ended with the sound of her name and his next kiss started in the hall, under the steady glare of a lone light bulb in the ceiling. It picked up momentum in the doorway to the madam's room and accelerated to dizzying proportions somewhere on the drop down to the mattress. The ancient springs creaked under the weight of two.

Slowly his mouth lifted from hers. His gaze traveled over her eyes, her mouth, the length of her curled next to him, back to her eyes. Desire was the hush of silence and the fierceness of a man's features who wanted, badly. His fingertip brushed her cheek with impossible gentleness, and then he reached behind him to undo the first tassel that tied the silk coverings around the bed. He undid the first, then the second, then the other two.

The light was still on in the hall, and that light shone through the silk, enclosed them in a blue world. Maggie's skin took on a fragile iridescence, and all Mike could think of was wanting to give her the kind of dreams she seemed to want so badly. "I didn't realize what this room would be like at night. This is a wicked bed, Maggie," Mike said slowly.

He wanted to talk? She was having trouble just breathing. "Yes."

"A very private bed. A pleasure bed."

"Yes."

"You can hear the river in here." He knelt over her, not touching. His thigh wasn't an inch from hers; the slightest movement would have brought her breasts in contact with his chest. He didn't touch. "You can imagine how dark that water is. Dark and soft, luring you in. You lure me in, Maggie. The touch of you lures me to take what I shouldn't take, want what I shouldn't want." He said softly, "Honey, if you're going to send me to the other room—do it now."

Perhaps he really believed he was giving her another chance to say no. She leaned on an elbow and let her fingers play over the line of his jaw, the smooth bone of his cheek, his furrowed brow. His eyebrows were an unmanageable shelf of short curling black hair. His nose she knew as well as her own. His lips . . . she just looked at his lips and knew what they felt like, tasted like.

One night might have been forgivable, her conscience warned her. But that same conscience hadn't absolved her for the night before. Good women didn't throw themselves at a man. Ever. No exceptions. He hadn't asked to make love to her last night. And this night, he hadn't said he loved her.

His need was a precious thing, though. More precious than any hidden treasures. She was a different woman than she'd been the night before. Yesterday's

Maggie had been caught up in fantasies. Yesterday that was all she believed she could ever have.

Tonight's Maggie was infinitely powerful. Fantasies could become real; there was the difference. It had to do with the river and the night and blue silk. It had to do with the way he'd taught her to make love. It had to do with the mystery of Michael, the brood behind his eyes, the way he avoided talk about his life, about himself. It was so simple. Mike was a man who needed someone and she was a woman who needed to give of herself.

She knelt in front of him, pushed up his sweater, drew it off. He wore a shirt beneath it. She unbuttoned the shirt, and when she reached bare skin, she stared with intimate approval. For now, for this moment, the smooth slope of his shoulder was hers. She touched with her fingertips, then with her lips.

The air hissed out of his lungs. "Are you trying to drive me over the edge?" he whispered.

"Could I do that?" Her eyes met his, hers open with sudden curiosity. "Could I do that to you, Mike?"

"Is that what you want to do?"

She hesitated. "Yes." She kissed his shoulder again, followed the line of his collarbone with her tongue. "Yes. Teach me," she whispered. "I want you to want so badly you could die for it. I want you to forget everything else, where we are, who I am, who you are. I want to lure you in, like ancient woman lured in her mate. And I want you to teach me . . . how to do all of that to you."

"God, Maggie. Stop it—"

"No." Her lips skimmed his collarbone, his throat, dipped into the nest of hair on his chest. His heartbeat wasn't the rhythm of a healthy man, but the beat of a man in stress. She gave him more stress. Her palm dropped to his knee and slowly, deliberately climbed his inner thigh. She traced the shape of him inside his jeans. Her fingertips found his waistband, slipped inside. Her lips never stopped moving. Her kisses wooed him shyly; her hands were wanton.

She changed that. Her fingertips turned teasing and light; her mouth sought his hungrily in the darkness.

And very suddenly she wasn't kneeling, but flat on her back. The look in Mike's eyes sent a shiver through her entire body. It was fierce and his voice was a rasping whisper. "You don't need to be taught anything, little one. Ever."

"I wasn't . . . finished."

"Yes, you were." He whispered, "You can't have everything your own way."

"Mike—"

"Hush, Maggie. It's your turn to teach me. What makes a woman feel wild with desire. Infinitely beautiful. Completely out of control. I'm going to drive you completely out of your mind, sweet . . ."

She was tempted to feel frightened. She seemed to have unleashed something that sent adrenaline pulsing through her blood, as if she were in danger. Danger was the sound of clothes dropping, the shadows of a man's mouth, lungs that kept forgetting to take in and let out air. Fear was the thread of pulse when he kissed behind her knee, her shoulder blade, her navel; he was that gentle. She felt that vulnerable.

Her skin turned into wet silk. She didn't recognize the sounds her lips made. Yearning started like a steady slow ache, became a storm of sweet pain. His lips courted the boundaries of sanity, crossed over to the other side. She asked to be taken; he denied her.

She asked again and again, until his name echoed in the darkness. Mike heard her. He cherished the whisper, savored it, used every skill he knew to tempt her further. There was no end to the sweetness in Maggie, no end to what he wanted for her. For months he'd felt lost as a man. For months his belief in himself had floundered. So much poured into his touch, the need to love, the need to touch and give again, all exploding because of Maggie. If she only knew the lover and not the man, if she only wanted the lover, that was all he would be for a time. All he needed to be. He felt alive loving her.

When he finally filled her, she felt as wild as wind, as hot as sun. She shifted, wanting him deeper yet, wanting to possess him, brand him. She wanted to yield, to drown him in softness. She wanted him all.

He gave her everything she wanted.

Hours later, years later, a lifetime later, she was exhausted; her whole body was still trembling, and there were tears of release in her eyes. "Nothing could ever—ever—be like that again," she whispered against his cheek.

He wrapped her close, nuzzled his lips to her damp forehead. "How the hell am I ever going to let you go,

Maggie?'' His voice was faint, low, distant, somehow angry.

"Mike?"

"Hush. Rest now."

Maggie burrowed away from the sudden harsh light. "No...wake up."

In the warmth of the sleeping bag, she sleepily reached for him. "It's cold. Where are you?" she murmured. "Come back here, Ianelli."

A rough hand shook her shoulder. "Come on. Wake up. Now."

She smiled, her eyes still closed. "I'll wake up," she promised groggily, "if you'll come back under the covers and..."

"Up! This isn't a game."

Her eyes shot open due to Mike's harsh tone. She winced, both from the sudden bright light and at the dark stranger glaring at her. Mike was dressed. Jeans, boots, jacket, everything. His mouth was set in a grim line. He wasn't the lover she'd slept with but the man she'd met in an airport, remote and broody and tight. "What's—?" Wrong, she started to say.

"We're going to be out of this place in five minutes flat." He tossed her her red sweater. It landed half on her head. Bending down, he snatched her jeans.

"What time is it?"

"Four. Your duffel bag's already in the car, and I've already taken care of the food. All you have to do is get dressed."

"Four in the *morning*?"

"The river's flooding. I shouldn't have fallen asleep. I never meant to. I meant to watch, because I knew damn well there was a chance of another storm...." He paced to the window, then back to her, then to the doorway again. "Five minutes. No more. Then you and I are leaving, and that's whether you've got your clothes on or not. Got that?"

She recognized that he was worried sick. She knew that he was angry at himself somehow for not staying awake. His sharp snap still chilled her. "Yes."

But he was gone. She burrowed into the jeans and sweater, her hands all thumbs at buttons and zippers; she was still half asleep. It took her an inordinately long time to locate her socks on the middle of the floor. River flooding? She pulled on the socks, ran her fingers through her hair, stood up and hurried for the bathroom.

"Maggie!"

She heard his impatient yell from below just as she was turning on the faucet on to splash cold water on her face. She splashed anyway. She couldn't have used up her five minutes already, and her body informed her she would be making a disastrous mistake not to pay a small visit to the gold leafed room marked LADIES.

He was holding her jacket for her when she stumbled down the stairs. She stepped into it, still trying to catch her breath. "My gloves—"

His quick smile never reached his eyes. "I found one, not the other. You have this small tendency to leave things all over the place. It doesn't matter. We're leaving. Now."

She parked both feet firmly. "Ianelli, you can stop yelling any time. I don't know what on earth you're even talking about—"

"I'm talking about a river flooding. I'm talking getting you out of here. And that I had no business letting last night happen!"

She swallowed that, which wasn't the easiest thing with the sudden huge lump in her throat. She vaulted ahead of him with chin high and eyes blurred. He was flicking off the last of the lights and she reached the outside door to the veranda first. She opened the door, took a step down, and gasped.

Five steps led down from the veranda. The bottom two were completely under water. The house was suddenly an island surrounded by a shallow lake of swirling, oil-dark water. It just wasn't possible. All she had to do was look up to see it wasn't possible. Trickles of spring soft rain drizzled down from the night sky; it was almost warm.

From behind her, Mike grabbed her around the ribs and lifted her. It wasn't the most romantic of carries, half on his shoulder and half dangling, but then he was trying to tote a bag in his other hand. "Hey—"

"The water'll be over your boots. Don't give me a hard time."

"But the house. What'll happen to the house?"

Mike had a short succinct word for what the house could do to itself.

Luckily the car was parked on higher ground. Maggie barely had time to notice that only the bottom edge of the tires were in water before she was stuffed into the passenger seat with the car door slammed in her ear. She had a minute before he was in the driver's seat. A minute to sort through confusion, groggy sleepiness, hurt from nowhere, and the glaze of a lover's dreams that still desperately wanted to linger.

When he stuck the key in the ignition, she said softly, "Hey. Lighten up, Ianelli. It's only a flood."

For an instant, a stark bare instant, she won one of his special smiles. "Sounds like Maggie the optimist just woke up."

"Is it really so terrible?" she insisted.

They were on the road long before the car's heater had a chance to work. "Your house will be fine," he assured her. "It was built for this. Not just the concrete foundation, but railroad support beams. Our grandfathers knew what they were doing and exactly where they were building. Not to worry."

"So why are you so...angry?"

He shot her a quick glance. "You could have been stranded there. I fell asleep. I knew what conditions were."

"So would I have...if you'd bothered to tell me," she said quietly. "Does Michael Ianelli always take on the world alone?" He didn't answer. Maggie guessed

he had no intention of answering. She asked, "Where
are we going?"

"The airport. There's no point going anywhere else.
There'll be no getting near the house for a while after
this." He added briskly, "I won't leave you until
you're safely on a plane to Philadelphia. I'm not
about to desert you in an airport in the middle of the
night."

She knew that. And rationally, she knew his hurry
had to do with floods and danger. Emotionally, she
felt the speed with which he was withdrawing from
her, from their weekend, from being part of her life.
She wished vaguely that she could dissolve.

The drive to the airport took an eternity...yet in far
too short a time, Mike was installing her in a plastic
seat next to her duffel bag while he went to see about
tickets. There wasn't a big rush for pre-dawn travel.
Within minutes he returned, carrying two cups of
black coffee, and dropped into the seat next to her.

"There's an hour to your flight."

"How much was the ticket?"

"We'll settle up another time."

She opened her mouth to object. She already had a
return ticket that was surely worth a partial refund.
Still, she said nothing. Mike's black eyes warned her.
Of what she wasn't sure.

They sat in silence, watching what few people wandered through the airport at that ungodly hour. Mike
said finally, "We'll have to settle the whole inheritance thing at another time. First of all, there isn't a
chance in hell of selling the house in these kinds of

conditions. Whistler told me the river only floods once every fifty years, but that hardly helps now."

"No."

"A month from now...no, two. April. The first weekend in April. That should guarantee us good weather conditions—in fact the best of conditions where we could really see all the place and grounds."

"Fine." A sip of coffee scalded her tongue. She was almost glad. The rest of her seemed increasingly numb.

"I'll pay Whistler's wages in the meantime."

"I'll share that." Mike's dark eyes soared on hers again. Another warning. This time she bristled. "I intend to share half of the expenses," she said firmly. "I don't know or care what you earn, Ianelli, so don't pull any macho business. I own half the place so I share half the expenses and that's that."

"We'll see. Don't get your Irish up about nothing, bright eyes."

That sounded like the Michael she thought she knew. For the first time since four that morning, she almost relaxed. Perversely, she felt like crying. It was over. Hurt was already setting in like a knife wound. He didn't care. She stared at the interesting swirls of black coffee in her cup for a very long time.

Mike's hand suddenly slipped between the fingers of her free hand. Palm to palm, she felt the warmth, the texture, the strength of him. She blinked tears back, fast.

"Flannery?"

"What?"

"Hey... please don't do that."

Men were such illogical creatures. They handled floods, then panicked because of a lone tear. For all he knew, she could have had a dust mote caught under her eyelid. "I'm just tired," she said crossly.

His hand tightened on hers, and his voice was low. "I didn't mean to be such a bastard, Maggie. All I could think of was you being stranded... and it being my fault." He added, "And that's no excuse." When she said nothing, he coaxed, "Would you kindly give me a smile so I can get out of hell?"

Her smile was watery. He wrapped an arm around her and tugged her close, oblivious of the partition between plastic chairs. The arm rest dug into her ribs. She kept her cheek right where it was, on his shoulder, until they called her flight.

He carried her duffel bag and jacket to the boarding gate. She walked with her hands slung in her pockets, and stole a glance at him, then another. They were meeting again in April, she'd heard that. That wasn't all she wanted to hear. She knew in her head she had no right to expect more, but her heart desperately wanted more.

The only other four passengers for the early-morning flight boarded first. Maggie didn't move. Something stubborn inside her wouldn't let her move, even when they called the last chance for boarding and the stewardess was cocking her head toward her curiously.

Mike handed her her jacket, then with a wry smile, her duffel tote. "You going to pack lighter in April?"

Yes, become a Silhouette subscriber and the celebratio goes on forever.

To begin with, we'll send you:

- 4 new Silhouette Desire novels—FREE
- an elegant, purse-size manicure set—FREE
- and an exciting mystery bonus—FREE

And that's not all! Special extras— three more reasons to celebrate.

4. Money-Saving Home Delivery. That's right! When you subscribe to Silhouette Desire, the excitement, romance and faraway adventures of these novels can be yours for previewing in the convenience of your own home. Here's how it works. Every month, we'll deliver six new books right to your door. If you decide to keep them, they'll be yours for only $1.95 each. That's 30¢ less per book than what you pay in stores. And there's **no charge for shipping and handling.**

5. Free Monthly Newsletter. It's the indispensable insider's look at our most popular writers and their up-coming novels. Now you can have a behind-the-scenes look at the fascinating world of Silhouette! It's an added bonus you'll look forward to every month!

6. More Surprise Gifts. Because our home subscribers are our most valued readers, we'll be sending you additional free gifts from time to time—as a token of our appreciation.

This beautiful manicure set will be a useful and elegant item to carry in your handbag. Its rich burgundy case is a perfect expression of your style and good taste. And it's yours free in this amazing Silhouette celebration!

SILHOUETTE DESIRE®

FREE OFFER CARD

4 FREE BOOKS

ELEGANT MANICURE SET —FREE

FREE MYSTERY BONUS

PLACE YOUR BALLOON STICKER HERE!

MONEY-SAVING HOME DELIVERY

FREE FACT-FILLED NEWSLETTER

MORE SURPRISE GIFTS THROUGHOUT THE YEAR—FREE

Yes! Please send me my four Silhouette Desire novels **FREE**, along with my manicure set and my **free mystery gift**. Then send me six new Silhouette Desire novels every month and bill me just $1.95 per book (30¢ less than retail), with no extra charges for shipping and handling. If I am not completely satisfied, I may return a shipment and cancel at any time. **The free books, manicure set and mystery gift remain mine to keep.**

CBD017

NAME _____
(PLEASE PRINT)

ADDRESS _____ APT. _____

CITY _____ STATE _____

ZIP _____

Terms and prices subject to change.
Your enrollment is subject to acceptance
by Silhouette Books.

PRINTED IN U.S.A.

FILL OUT THIS POSTPAID CARD AND MAIL TODAY!

Postage will be paid by addressee

BUSINESS REPLY MAIL
FIRST CLASS PERMIT NO. 194 CLIFTON, N.J.

SILHOUETTE BOOKS
120 Brighton Road
P.O. Box 5084
Clifton, NJ 07015-9956

NO POSTAGE
NECESSARY
IF MAILED
IN THE
UNITED STATES

"I'd like to say yes, but I doubt it."

"You can call someone to help you manage when you get home?"

She nodded, knowing she'd manage well alone. A part of Maggie had always managed alone and this was no different...except that it was totally different. "Well," she said brightly, "I guess this is—"

She stopped talking when he abruptly snatched the duffel bag right out of her hand again. It thudded to the floor, about the same instant his arms went around her. Warm lips homed in on hers. She knew that kiss. Her lips were labeled Mike's; she felt his hands in her hair. The hard length of him deliberately pressed against her.

When he finally released her mouth, his breath fanned close to hers and his pure black eyes were only inches away. They were sexier than the devil's, twice as dangerous. "Don't be an ass, Flannery. You don't think for a moment I could ever forget you? You think for one instant you aren't the most special woman I've ever met?"

Another kiss, a swift possessive kiss. Then her gear was being handed back to her and he was gone.

She couldn't watch him walk away because the stewardess was beckoning impatiently toward her. Minutes later, she was strapped in for takeoff. The pilot droned his welcome and promise of a smooth flight on the intercom. Maggie closed her eyes, oblivious.

Later, she realized that she didn't know what he did for a living, or where he lived, or even whether there was another woman in his life. She knew absolutely nothing about the stranger she'd met on the river, except his name. And that she'd fallen in love with him.

"I wish you didn't have to rush off so quickly after dinner, darling. I feel like I've hardly seen you in the last three weeks. You never did tell me much about that little trek you took to . . ."

"Indiana," Maggie supplied for her mother.

Barbara Flannery smiled vaguely—Indiana was too far from Philadelphia to worry about remembering—and slipped an arm around her youngest daughter's waist as they walked to the living room. "Kind of a resort sort of place, didn't you tell me? I was never surprised he left it to you, sweetheart. You were always your grandfather's favorite."

Maggie perched on the arm of a sofa, talking family gossip and clothes and her mother's theater group, at the same time her eyes wandered over the living room. Medieval music was Barbara's latest fad; the muted wail of mandolins and lutes came from unseen speakers in the far corners. In her mother's latest decorating venture, the carpeting was stark black and the furniture white, making a backdrop for the dizzying geometric designs that graced the walls. Last year her mother had favored Monet.

Mike would have taken one look and winced, Maggie mused fleetingly and immediately drowned the thought.

"I really can't stay," she said lightly. "I'm afraid I brought a briefcase full of work home from the office tonight."

"You're so busy, darling," Barbara said affectionately. She never simply sat down, she swept into a chair as she did now, crossing the long elegant legs that she'd failed to pass on to her daughter. Her hair was still a vibrant red, unlike Maggie's subdued auburn, and her vivid red and scarlet print dress was in direct contrast to her daughter's dove-gray business suit. The shrewd eyes that studied her daughter were full of approval in spite of the obvious differences between the women. "Sure you wouldn't like a quick drink?"

"No, but thanks."

Again, Barbara looked pleased, and Maggie knew exactly what was going through her mother's head because she'd heard the words spoken a dozen times before. Her brother Blake had a "slight problem" with drinking, just as Justin had a "slight problem" staying away from a party. Her sister Andrea had a "slight problem" going through men, and Maggie's father had a "slight problem" holding onto money. It was a godsend he had the ability to make it as well. All together, the immediate family, as well as the tag ends of aunts and uncles and cousins that clanned together at every holiday for an uproariously good time, was rather loaded with "slight problems."

Only Maggie had been tagged perfect, and she expected the honorary maternal questions. "Your job's still going well, isn't it?"

"Just fine."

"I never asked you if you were still dating that man who was once a seminary student—"

"He was just a good friend."

"But a good man," Barbara said gently, and smiled. "Never mind, I'll stop prying. You handle your life so well, Margaret Mary. If I haven't told you in a long time, I'm ridiculously proud of you."

For the smallest instant, Maggie hesitated. If she told her mother that her life was a disaster, she knew Barbara would instantly rally for her, but the habit of pride was too hard to bridge. She'd never burdened her mother before and wasn't about to risk disappointing her now.

She escaped around nine, and drove home to her apartment through a crisp, cold March night, letting fatigue wash over her like a welcome friend. Perhaps, if she were tired enough, she would sleep tonight. She hadn't slept well in the past three weeks.

Inside her apartment foyer, she fumbled in her purse for the mailbox key. Claiming her stack of mail, she filtered through it as she mounted the three steps up to her apartment door.

The first week after she'd gotten home from Indiana, she'd raced for the mail the instant she came home from work. Still, she understood why there'd been no letter from Mike. He'd just gotten home; they'd just seen each other.

The second week, she'd made herself wait before going to the mailbox. If she didn't hurry, something would be there. If she had dinner first, something would be there. If she were a paragon of virtue at work . . . but there was never anything in the box. And cutting telephone calls short to ensure the line was free didn't produce any extra calls.

Now she was immune. The man had promised her nothing and committed nothing. So what if he'd said some pretty words at the last minute at the airport. She wasn't hurt. She'd given herself freely with no regrets.

She pushed open her apartment door, still sifting through the phone bill, the electric bill, the letter from Justin, two junk mail catalogs. Her fingers closed instinctively on the small envelope with a San Francisco stamp. One immune heart suddenly remembered how to beat again.

Still, she pushed off her coat, kicked off her shoes, and curled up in the coral rocker in her living room before she allowed a forefinger to slip beneath the glued section of the envelope. There was nothing inside but a small slip of paper.

"Maggie, hope the first weekend in April is still all right with you? The only way I'm reachable—temporarily—is through the enclosed post office box. Have rethought our white elephant. Will have news for you when I see you."

She read the note twice, then let it slip to her lap. The missive was friendly and informative. Her boss or her next door neighbor could have written it.

Just maybe, she told herself, it's time to face reality. She turned her attention to her living room. It hadn't taken her a fortune to furnish it, just a great deal of time to find exactly the shade of coral she loved. The serene feminine shade was everywhere, complemented only by a spray of green plants and an occasional ivory ornament. She loved ivory. She'd always loved her apartment.

Funny, that it smothered her at the moment. Ianelli, you are a heartless user, she thought.

Only he wasn't.

She was the one who'd brazenly thrown herself at him without a hint of love or commitment. Mike had been nothing but honest with her. In fact, he'd carefully made sure she knew that his feelings didn't include love. A lonely, troubled man had simply taken what a woman had freely offered him. How could she blame him? And in the meantime she wasn't hurting.

No, she was dying. She bit her lip, swallowed the damn tears and surged to her feet. She had a cup to wash out, plants to water, any number of incredibly important things demanding her immediate attention.

Her first priority—the only thing she had to do before seeing him again in April—was toughen up, learn to be a realist like Ianelli. For two short days in February, she'd believed that two very different people had something very special together. She knew better now.

Believing in fantasies was dangerous. It was a mistake Maggie never intended to make again.

Six

The Indianapolis office building could have existed in any major city—it had a lot of glass, a lot of concrete, piped-in music and an attractive woman sitting at the reception desk.

The eleventh floor held executive offices. The largest suite was tastefully decorated to promote serene and quiet working conditions. The pecan-colored walls worked beautifully against textured paneling and thick toast-colored carpet. The man behind the expansive desk did not have the word "serenity" in his vocabulary, however, nor did he give a hoot in hell about textured paneling.

Mike expected exactly what he got. George Saxton was fifty-five. Except for a few wisps of hair around his ears he was bald. Shrewd eyes glared over a crooked nose, and the huge husky frame matched his natural bark of a voice. "You barged your way in here under false pretenses—"

"Yes. There was no other way to see you." Mike, standing in front of the pecan desk, showed no trace of nerves. In a gray business suit, he looked strong and tall and in command. He wasn't here to beg. His quiet voice had intimidated enough people to get him in here, although—and he wanted it that way—it had no effect on Saxton. "I have the qualifications for the job you have available in your financial department. More than that, I specifically want to work with you."

Saxton's eyes narrowed on the "with" that should have been a respectful "for." "Then you're wasting my time and yours. All jobs are handled first through personnel. No exceptions. I haven't seen line one of your references—"

"Which is why I came directly to you, Mr. Saxton." Mike dropped a file on the desk. "I was fired from my last job. There was a suggestion that I'd mishandled funds. If your personnel department had called my former employer for a reference, I have no doubt he'd have told them that I'm an out and out thief."

George Saxton never showed surprise, but he found himself momentarily leaning back. Black eyes met gray squarely. For those long seconds neither backed down, but when Saxton spoke again his tone held as much curiosity as irritation. "Then what the hell made you believe I'd even look at you twice for the job?"

Mike didn't hesitate. "I did a little homework before I came here. You bought this company when it was in Chapter 7, and you put it back in the black with lots of guts and a minimum of capital. You've also done it before—once, with a manufacturing company in Dayton, and a second time in Cincinnati. That's what you like to do—buy a company, turn it around, and then leave it in capable hands while you're on to the next challenge. You've been frustrated trying to find someone to leave this child of yours with." Mike added swiftly, aware Saxton was becoming impatient, "You also have three daughters; you like to travel; and you're originally from Boston. At Brown University, you roomed with a man named Jason Stuart."

Mike waited, and then played his last card, his only ace. "If you'll look inside that file, you'll see that I worked for Stuart-Spencer in San Francisco. Jason Stuart was my boss. The man you roomed with." Only the faintest pallor beneath Mike's coloring revealed that this interview meant anything to him. That, and the stark honesty in his last admission. "I'm here because you're exactly the kind of man I want to work with. Because the job is exactly suited to what I want to do. And because I believed you might know what kind of man Jason Stuart was—and is."

Silence. The older man didn't open the file; he just studied Mike. Seconds ticked by, each longer than the last.

Abruptly a hard calloused hand extended across the desk. "Don't think for a minute I won't work your ass off," Saxton said flatly. "And if you're working for me, Ianelli, you might as well start right now."

It was nine hours later before Mike climbed back in his car. A March wind blew cold and wild. It was nearing midnight, and his car was alone in the parking lot. Leaning back in the seat, he closed his eyes and controlled himself from letting out an exultant roar that would wake up a sleepy Indianapolis. Dammit, he wished Maggie were at his side.

He'd left her six weeks ago to the day, six weeks in which every waking moment had been spent turning his life around. None of that was for Maggie, it was something he had to do for himself. But the courage to seek out this specific job in spite of impossible odds had come from a green-eyed woman from Philadelphia...a woman who'd taken on a stranger, foolishly believed in him and blindly given herself with love.

A dozen times he'd nearly picked up the phone to call her and hadn't. Initially he felt he had no right to call without a prayer of a future to offer her, but there was more to it than a man's feelings of failure for being out of work. He'd written Maggie one carefully worded note, and knew when he returned to his motel room that he'd write her another equally careful missive, letting her know his change of address and affirming their meeting in early April—but nothing more.

He owed Maggie for believing in him when he'd all but stopped believing in himself, and he owed her for that unselfish love she'd given so freely. He owed her enough to make sure she had time and choices. Mike was ruthlessly honest with himself. Maggie may well not want to hear from him. She doesn't even know you, Ianelli. She needed a stranger and you were there. Those were two stolen days that she probably wants to forget. Just a fantasy for her.

Dammit, the first weekend in April seemed an eternity away.

The woman reflected in the tiny oval mirror looked every inch a lady. Maggie flicked the compact closed and leaned back as the plane descended. The landing was as smooth as glass and couldn't possibly be held accountable for the queasy flipflop of her stomach.

The jet rolled to a stop. Seat belts clicked open right and left; briefcases and small bags were retrieved from overhead storage compartments. Maggie discovered her fanny didn't want to unglue itself from the seat. It was very nice on the plane. Safe. The temperature was lovely. The food had been almost edible. When she'd left home two hours earlier, it had seemed terribly important that she see Mike again—to show him that she had pride, and to prove to herself that loving him had never been more than an illusion.

At the moment, it seemed a much better idea to simply return home. Hiding in the bathroom struck her as another intelligent option. Continuing on to St. Louis with the plane was a third choice. In fact, the only rotten idea in the bunch was deplaning and having to face Ianelli.

She sighed, unhooked her seat belt, and stood up.

Mike scanned the airport crowd, his hands on his jeaned hips as the flight from Philadelphia deplaned. An elderly woman got off, then three men in business suits, then a young woman looking harried and carrying a whining two year old. Impatiently he shifted on his feet. Where was the lady with the flyaway red hair and endless green eyes?

Anxiety creased a frown on his forehead. She wasn't coming. Something had happened. For weeks he'd been afraid that something would happen and she wouldn't—or couldn't—come. Or that she'd left him and found someone else back home—someone who had more to offer her than fantasies, and who'd have the sense not to let her get away the first time. The little hammer in his head had been tapping that refrain for days now.

A towheaded boy ambled off the plane, then an attractive woman in a pale green suit with her hair twisted in back. His eyes whisked past her, then homed in again. His right eyebrow arched in surprise. He hadn't expected her to look so cool and efficient. Perhaps he should have. He hadn't anticipated the flawlessly applied makeup, or that she was almost striking in business clothes and wasn't such a sprite in high heels. Her eyes were the same, though. He'd counted on those green eyes, and as soon as they made contact he surged forward with a smile.

All right, you knew his smiles could make a nun's blood pressure rise. You knew those dark eyes would remind you of the madam's room. Just smile, Margaret Mary. She smiled.

Her eyes had to slowly go over him once, just to make sure he'd been happy and well. Not because she still cared, but strictly out of curiosity.

Obviously, he'd thrived without her. A few added pounds didn't change the basic lean look, but his jeans molded just a little tighter over well-muscled thighs and his dark sweatshirt strained to fit his shoulders. That haunted tension had been replaced by a cocky stride and an aura of power and confidence.

His mouth hadn't changed. It was still dangerous to any woman within a five-mile radius. His cheekbones still jutted arrogantly; his nose was still straight; and his dark eyes still had the power to rip a sane woman's moorings loose and promote naughty fantasies.

But not for her, not anymore. She parked herself a safe foot away. "Hi, Mike."

The cool greeting appeared to make him hesitate, but only for seconds. "I was getting worried you'd missed the flight." He cocked his head, dark eyes dancing. "Looking pretty sexy there, Flannery. Almost didn't recognize you."

"No?" Again, she smiled politely. "I went straight from work to the airport; there was no time to change."

"Your flight go okay?" He glanced down, then shot her a grin as he reached for her green Samsonite bag. "Hey, what is this? Where's our duffel bag that broke my back the last time?"

That "our" whispered across her nerves like velvet on silk. Temptation, she discovered, was a simple three letter word. On her last run-in with temptation, she hadn't had the self-preservation instincts of a goose. Now, she applauded herself for being smarter. "I figured it was about time I learned to pack light." She moved briskly ahead of him. "I gathered from your notes that you've moved from California?"

"Yes." His job was nothing he wanted to get into yet. He ducked around two chattering women to open the door ahead of her. "You're not going to believe the place in springtime. Trees are in flower all over the place. The river looks like an idyllic stream. You'd never believe it was capable of flooding."

When that got no response, he added, "I haven't had much time to work on it, but I tackled a few things. The roof had a small leak, nothing major. A little cleaning, a little rewiring—" He shot her another grin. "There's hot water now, believe it or not."

A faint warm breeze danced over her skin outside. The sun wasn't hot, but trying. The whole damn world smelled of spring, she thought irritably. "I've come prepared to work. Whatever we need to do to get the place in shape to sell."

"Yes, well…" Cars were darting here and there. He instinctively reached for her arm, and perplexed, felt her stiffen. His hand dropped. He smiled again, a little more carefully. "The car's this way. Maggie, we both knew you took one look at the place and never really wanted to sell it. I've been looking into that thought you had, about converting it into a business retreat—"

"Ridiculous idea, wasn't it? You must have thought I was crazy," she said smoothly. "Not to worry, I'm not normally so impractical or impulsive. My whole life's set up in Philadelphia; I can't imagine what I was thinking of. Of course we'll sell it, just like you wanted to to begin with.''

She caught his long, slow look, then heard as well as felt the car door close quietly. The breeze fingered through his hair, flattened the sweatshirt against his skin as he crossed in front of the car. He looked cool, in control, a self-assured man who could take anything life handed out and give it back in spades.

A small voice whispered in her head, don't hurt him. The voice came from nowhere, the thought was totally illogical, and Maggie schooled herself against any more imaginative instincts. Besides, she had no intention of hurting him. Mike wasn't her enemy; she'd been her own enemy. All she wanted was to keep her distance from him.

Mike climbed in the driver's side of the Pontiac, then stretched up to dig in the front pocket of his jeans for the key. ''I originally thought that selling it was the only option,'' he admitted slowly. ''Until I looked into your idea. Indianapolis couldn't be more centrally located between cities of all sizes—Louisville, Cincinnati, Dayton, St. Louis, Gary, Cleveland. It's only a few hours drive from all of them. Like you said, both small and big businesses believe in educating their managers these days, and the tendency is to combine that with stress-free time. Your idea of providing a place to hold seminars—''

"Might have some merit. And maybe whoever we sell it to can follow through with that, if they like." She smiled.

He smiled back.

He started the car. The engine reliably vibrated to life. It was still a sunny afternoon in Indianapolis. The road was predictably a nuisance of Friday afternoon traffic. There was no reason to feel like someone had just socked him in the gut.

Maybe she was tired, he thought fleetingly. Maggie certainly had a right to be tired. She also had a right to be different than he remembered her. Dammit, he'd never expected her to take one look and just fall into his arms again.

He hadn't *expected* that, but he'd wanted it. He'd wanted to tease her about packing the kitchen sink; he'd wanted those lush green eyes to sneak looks at him; he'd wanted to make her feel easy, because the Maggie he knew would have been nervous about meeting him again. He'd wanted her to just slightly irritate him when she was too optimistic and too inclined to put her head in a cloud; he'd wanted . . .

He stole a glance at her hands. The nails on two fingers were bitten to the quick. That was Maggie. On the next turn, he risked a glance at her chest. Flat. That was Maggie, too. And the spring wind had loosened the smooth coil of her hair; fine wisps of silky auburn curled around her chin, so like Maggie. He caught only an instant of bright green eyes, too bright, vulnerably bright, before her lashes shuttered down.

You hurt her, you bastard. The thought came like a bullet, sharp, fast, and cold.

"Maggie?"

"Hmmm?"

His voice could have rolled onto cotton-fluff without denting it, his tone was so careful, so slow and testing. "Whether you believe it or not, I almost called you a hundred times. There was a reason why I—"

"Hey, I didn't expect a call. I got your notes. There was really nothing we could do about the place until we saw it together again, now was there?" she said blithely. She leaned over to roll down the window part way. "Philadelphia's greened up but not like this. Spring really hits with a vengeance in Indiana, I take it?"

"Yes." So, he thought fiercely. So what? So he should have called her. His head informed him promptly that he should have done a hell of a lot more than call her. Only how was he supposed to explain to her about a man and his pride? What if she didn't care to hear?

So, she thought fiercely. Check out my skin, Ianelli. Very thick. Nothing dents any more. You won't have to worry about a flat-chested redhead throwing herself at you this time.

Mike took the fast lane on the expressway, his foot clamped on the accelerator. She never really wanted you, Ianelli.

You were never in love with him, she thought, and was promptly irritated with herself. "In love" was one of those phrases she'd drilled out of her vocabulary.

"With the weather so different, we'll have a lot easier weekend than we did last time," Mike said flatly.

"Much easier," Maggie concurred.

Dangerous thoughts tried to assail her when Mike pulled off onto the last stretch of narrow road. Memories started ticking off one after the other... the rutted road, the tangle of branches that brushed against the side of the car, then the small stone bridge and tall wrought iron gates. Civilization disappeared behind them. The feeling of a lonely road going nowhere hit like an unwelcome déjà vu and mixed with an anticipation she didn't want to feel toward seeing the house again.

She squelched those feelings, of course, but Ianelli didn't help matters when he rolled down his window. Where she'd noticed the sameness, now the differences assaulted her senses. She could suddenly smell hyacinths and lilacs. Overgrown, droopy dogwoods wandered between the mammoth oaks and maples. The acres of lawn were spring green and smelled just mowed and impossibly fresh. The river in the distance gurgled like a baby's laughter, innocent and carefree.

And the house loomed there so suddenly. Mike stopped the car and glanced at her as he reached for her green suitcase. "Like you remembered?"

"No, not really." It was actually exactly as she remembered, from the madam's room jutting over the river to the cool dark veranda that still echoed laughter from too long ago.

If anything, the draw of the house was even more fierce now than the first time. It was still a house of pleasure, a house of dreams; now Maggie had received a taste of both. The reality of seeing it again was bittersweet. If her own foolish fantasies had irreparably hurt her, yearnings didn't disappear any easier than love did. It was a house that craved love, life, laughter.

"I figured you'd be hungry by the time we arrived. This time we've got a reasonably stocked kitchen."

"Do we?"

"I didn't move to the area until a month ago. For now, I'm camped out in a company condominium, but I've been half living here while I did repairs the last few weekends."

She stepped inside and blinked against the sudden cool darkness after the brilliant afternoon sunshine. Her gaze skimmed over the newly varnished floors, windows that sparkled, marble that gleamed from the fireplaces. The cobwebs had disappeared from the corners; the smell of dust was completely gone. She noted all of this in one long startled glance, but her eyes landed unerringly on a simple water glass in the windowsill.

The glass was filled with wild flowers. Brown-eyed Susans and daisies and even bright yellow dandelions.

A lump formed in her throat, about four miles thick and six miles wide.

Mike rubbed a sore nerve at the back of his neck, unsure why she'd stopped dead in the center of the room but well aware of his failure to fix things up, female-style. "Take a look at the kitchen?" he suggested.

Maggie dragged her eyes away from the flowers, and moved swiftly toward the doorway. "Sure."

Mike trailed behind her. "Maggie, I couldn't tackle much in the house without talking changes over with you first. I had a woman come in here for a couple of days—just to clean."

"I can see." The windows sparkled; all the cupboards and walls had been washed. Maggie had loved the character of the kitchen from the first time she'd laid eyes on it, but that wasn't what she noticed now. On the counter by the sink were three bunches of bananas, Maggie's brand of coffee, an assortment of dried fruit, and worse, several pounds of butterscotch candies. Dammit. How could he?

Mike, his hands jammed in his pockets then leaned against the doorway, assailed again by uneasiness at her silence. "Now, I thought an awful lot about this room, because it's the only place in the house that needs serious work done to it. I suppose I could have started tearing the place up—"

"Tearing it up!" Maggie whirled on him, the lump in her throat temporarily receding in response to sheer horror. "Nothing in this room needs tearing up, Ianelli!"

His jaw, by a miracle, didn't sag in shock. "Maggie, the whole kitchen is old-fashioned, completely inefficient. I guess I automatically figured—"

"It's a country kitchen; it's not supposed to be efficient. I mean, yes, there's room for an island counter in here and better lighting. That would 'efficient' things up, but they don't even build kitchens with counter space and cupboards like this any more. You put checked curtains in windows like those, plants on the sill; you hang up copper pots—I mean," Maggie amended hastily, "whoever buys it would do that kind of thing. If they had any sense."

"If they had any sense," Mike echoed, and suddenly stroked the bridge of his nose. "I had no idea about those copper pots, but anyway...it's not salable *or* livable without doing a little something. The linoleum's all pitted...."

"I know." Maggie frowned, studying. "Still, a woman can't pick out linoleum for another woman's kitchen."

"No? I mean no," Mike agreed sagely. "But if we had to do something to just make it salable—"

"Blue." The word just slipped out.

"To go with the blue-and-white-striped curtains?"

"Checked curtains, Ianelli. Or chintz. Not stripes." Men.

Mike could care less about curtains. He saw the first dent in her cool brisk armor and every instinct told him to go with it. "Of course," he said casually, "if some kind of institution bought the place, they might want to use a lot of chrome. Chrome counters and sink—what's wrong?''

"No chrome.'' Was he deliberately trying to make her ill?

"Ah, well. . . .'' Mike cleared his throat. "We could talk about the house a little later, Maggie. Why don't you get into more comfortable clothes? I can have dinner half-ready by the time you change.''

"Fine.''

Getting away from the man struck her as the best idea since cotton candy. She grabbed her overnight case and hurried up the stairs, furious with herself. Somewhere, in a very nasty part of her unconscious, she seemed to have harbored a few fantasies about cooking dinners for Ianelli in that damn kitchen.

She'd banned all conscious fantasies. Unconscious ones were a little rougher to deal with. You're going to have to get a lot tougher than this, she scolded herself. Tough, realistic. Strong like rock.

Only she didn't feel much like a rock when she popped her head into the madam's room. Clearly, Mike intended her to sleep here. The windows had been opened and a cool, fragrant spring breeze rushed off the river. Powder-blue sheets were made up on the bed, and topped with a pure white comforter.

She set her case down with a thump on the love seat. The flowers, the butterscotch candies, the fluff of a white down comforter. He'd done a few considerate things. No, he'd done some unbelievably special things. That really wasn't fair.

It didn't, however, change two months of silence. The man was just being nice to a woman he'd shared a couple of nights with. What'd she expect him to do, treat her like a stranger? You can't treat anyone like a stranger when you know they have a tiny mole on the inside of their right thigh. She knew he had a scar on his left one.

A scar she'd do well to completely forget. She slipped out of her suitcoat and skirt. From her suitcase, she drew out tan jeans, a striped shirt in various shadows of brown, and a bulky white sweater.

Dressed, with her hair tamed back into a twist again, she wandered back downstairs…and found no one, either in the surrounding rooms or the kitchen. A fork was lying on the counter, also a brown cork, and the back door was ajar.

"Out here, Maggie!"

Seven

Pied Piper style, Maggie trailed outside to the sound of Mike's voice. The sun was just edging down over the trees, and he had made a firepit of stones on a little peninsula of land that jutted out into the river. Flames leaped up, dancing against the last rays of sunlight, illuminating the face of the man who turned to her, all dark eyes and the devil's lazy smile. "I got a little carried away with the firewood. Might be just a little longer before we can actually cook the steaks."

Maggie saw the steaks, the foil-wrapped potatoes, the butterscotch candies, and felt herself stiffen. They'd had the exact same meal by firelight before. "I want to thank you...for going to so much trouble for a place for me to sleep," she told him politely.

He considered grabbing her, kissing her senseless, and permanently wiping off that polite smile. Instead, he motioned her down to the blanket he'd spread out, reached for the opened bottle of champagne, and poured it into two paper cups with trivia questions printed on the side. "You told me you had insomnia when you traveled, Maggie, remember? Only I thought you might like the taste of this better than your Irish Whiskey," he said lightly and handed her a cup. "Shall we toast our den of iniquity?"

Her throat was suddenly dry. Mike remembered too much. All the little things. Why are you doing this to me, Ianelli? "A great idea," she said brightly.

"To the den." He touched her cup.

"To the den." The cool liquid shivered all the way down her throat; her tongue tingled with it.

Before she'd swallowed, Mike was touching her glass again. "To sin," he said smoothly. "If I remember right, you insisted on that toast last time, Flannery." His eyes dared her to deny it.

She couldn't. There seemed a lot of things she couldn't suddenly deny. Shadows crackled in the woods. Next to them she could hear the soft lap lap lap of the river. In February, she'd never once seen the sky, the clouds had never cleared away long enough. Now the sky was clear and shaded in that incredible deep blue that appeared just before night fell. Stars were already winking on the river like diamond promises. Mike was close enough to touch, close enough that she could breathe him in. And he kept looking at her.

The pulse in her throat refused to stop beating. She'd thought she had more pride than to talk herself into the illusion of loving him and feeling loved.

Yet it would not be difficult to reach for the forbidden again. Sin was as easy as the temptation to live for the moment, and not care about the future, just as their grandfathers had done. Mike's eyes held the invitation.

An invitation to sex, Margaret Mary, not love, her conscience warned her. And that's exactly where you misunderstood everything before. You bounced in bed shamelessly fast, so don't blame him for expecting you to be just that available. It's up to you to show him you don't believe in fantasies any more.

"Another cup of champagne?" he asked.

She shook her head. "That's more than enough for me. What can I do to help here?"

"Nothing...but be here."

The fire quieted at the same time the sun dipped in the horizon. The sky was suddenly as golden and orange and scarlet as the coals, and the hush of darkness slowly enveloped the woods and grounds behind them.

Mike dropped down beside her when he handed her her steak. Sitting Indian style, his knee touched hers whenever either of them moved. He draped his jacket over her shoulders when a chill breeze quickened off the river, and the jacket smelled of old leather and Mike. The light wind tugged at her hair, loosening a strand around her cheek. When she went to push it back, his fingers were already there, gently curling the strand behind her ear. "You're not eating," he scolded. "You need your steak cooked a little longer?"

"It's fine." Perfect in fact. The steak she'd cooked for them a long time ago had been raw, and if she could just manage to forget that steak, perhaps she could manage to eat this one. "Mike, we need to talk about selling the place," she said desperately.

When dinner was over, Mike pushed closer a fallen log to use as a backrest. "You're absolutely sure you don't even want to discuss keeping it?" he asked quietly.

"Positive," she agreed, and then hesitated. "Unless you want it, of course. If you want it—"

"Not alone, no. The upkeep would be impossible and it would be pointless for one person to live here." He waited an imperceptible second. His options seemed to be falling away, one by one. She appeared immune to memories of their time together before, immune to him. For those short minutes in the kitchen, he thought he'd caught a glimpse of the old Maggie, and could have sworn she still had a love for the house. Now he groped for something to hold her with. "If you're sure you don't want anything to do with it, I'll handle the sale," he said flatly.

"We could see a real estate agent tomorrow morning," she pressed.

"We could." He leaned back against the log. As fast as he stretched out his long legs, she curled hers up beneath her. When his arm almost touched her hand, she managed to be three inches out of reach before he'd even seen her move. "But I had other plans for tomorrow, Maggie. I can see a realtor on Monday, and this is something I thought you'd rather do."

"What?" she asked curiously.

He really didn't have the least idea, but his mind was whirling at seventy miles an hour, trying to think of something—anything—that would recapture her interest. "I was waiting to see you before telling you that I'd come up with some old history on the place, and for that matter, some information on your grandfather's treasure."

She was already shaking her head when he went on smoothly, "The caretaker led me on to an old woman who used to work here during our grandfathers' time. I thought we'd go see her tomorrow. Seems the Flannery-Ianelli partnership folded rather promptly when the prohibition law was repealed, but that didn't necessarily mean the house was empty."

Maggie's brows formed feathery wings. "Someone else lived here?"

"Lived here, no. Hid out here, perhaps." Mike leaned forward to start scattering the fire. "Seems Dillinger was terrorizing the Midwest, robbing banks around that time—we're talking 1933-34. All the empty speakeasies that died out with the end of prohibition made ideal potential hideouts for him. The law caught up with him in 1934, a year after liquor was made legal again, but the lady I met claims the government never recovered the mass bulk of the bank loot. She says there has to be a fortune still stashed somewhere along this river."

He glanced at Maggie and caught the unwilling sparkle of interest in her eyes. Against the fire, her hair looked a blend of russet and dark gold, and her skin had the glow of softness. He wanted that glow to be for him, not for romantic images of bootleggers, treasures and a fanciful past.

He'd never meant to bring the subject up. Wanting nothing more than to be totally honest with Maggie, he never believed a word of those stories. All his life he'd prided himself on being a man of integrity. A man of integrity didn't use a lady's imagination against her.

Abruptly, he felt an ironic kinship with his grandfather. Integrity *was* amazingly easily jettisoned when a man's ship was floundering. If it took fantasies to bring on her smiles again, he'd used them. And if it took the magnetic draw she'd once felt for a stranger, he'd be that stranger again for her.

"That's nonsense," Maggie said swiftly. "I never really believed there was treasure in the house, and neither did you."

"Your grandfather must have meant something in the letter he left you."

"Gramps could have meant sunshine. Grass. You didn't know him."

"No," Mike agreed. He only knew the granddaughter. A woman once crazy enough to get excited about a moth-eaten feather boa. A woman once trusting enough to assume she was safe with a stranger for a weekend. A woman loving enough to make a cynical man want to cherish her. Mike delved in his pocket, and palm out, handed her a butterscotch. His eyes met hers. So you don't believe in treasure any more, Maggie? But somehow I'm going to make you believe I never meant to hurt you.

He said, "The old biddy I told you about? She claims the fortune Dillinger left was in gold bullion. And that the government is still offering a reward for that unrecovered bank money. We could at least go and see her, Maggie. Wouldn't you at least get a kick out of meeting someone who knew your grandfather back then?"

"Perhaps, but I really don't think—?" She couldn't finish the thought. Mike had unwrapped the butterscotch and leaned closer. The tips of his fingers traced her mouth, coaxing her lips to separate. For that instant, she felt surrounded by Mike, by the virility implicit in his touch, the warmth of his skin, the closeness of his eyes. The sweet taste of the candy exploded on her tongue. She forgot Dillinger, treasures, speakeasies. Silver brushed her skin wherever he looked at her, and the taste of butterscotch was the forbidden sweet flavor of a man's kisses a long time ago.

"We'll go see her tomorrow together," Mike murmured.

She shook her head. He didn't seem to see; he'd turned away, was standing to douse the last of the fire. "I'll get the tray, if you'll bring the blanket. It's late. About time we got you settled in for the night."

"Mike—" Grabbing the blanket, she whisked the dirt scraps from it and folded it as she trailed after him toward the back door.

"I'm staying with you over the weekend," he called over his shoulder.

She missed a step. "I thought you said—"

"Yes. I've got temporary digs in town. Only you're not staying alone here in the middle of nowhere without even a phone." His tone was flat, begging for an argument.

Maggie was smarter than to give him one. Emotions inevitably flared in arguments, and that was a risk she didn't want to take. Besides, she trusted him. Mike had never taken what wasn't freely offered. "That would be fine," she said evenly as they reached the door. "Surely you didn't think I had any objections if you slept here?"

Perhaps she misunderstood, but she could have sworn that the tension eased just slightly from his shoulders. "I'll sleep in the green room," he said brusquely.

That lone admission told Maggie that he'd originally intended something else. Color flew to her cheeks. She ducked in ahead of him, aware that his dark eyes had immediately pounced on that unwilling flush. Inside the kitchen, she immediately slipped his jacket off and hooked it on the nearest chair. "Good thing you're staying," she said lightly. "You can watch for the bats."

There, a smile. A real one. An F. Michael Ianelli intimate special. Maggie's breath caught in her throat, as if she'd been waiting for one of those for hours. "I'll watch for all the monsters, Flannery," he said softly. "And if you call out, believe me I'll be there."

Sleepy-eyed, Maggie regarded the contents of her suitcase with a frown. Morning sun shimmered through the windows behind her in long yellow waves. Birds outside were going insane for spring. The river splish-splashed right below her window. All of this was very nice, but she'd forgotten to bring a towel, washcloth, or soap.

This time she'd been determined to pack light. Her duffel bag had earned her nothing but a teasing last time. Intelligent women thought less of packing bananas and more of packing makeup. She'd packed makeup, and spent an inordinate amount of time choosing her clothes, like the trim white jeans and figure-concealing green sweater she was wearing. Only where was her toothpaste?

She peeked outside the madam's room, and neither heard nor saw a sound coming from the closed door to the green room. Tiptoeing across the hall, she pushed open the door to the bathroom.

"Morning, Maggie."

Her heart just about jumped out of her chest. "Good morning. I didn't mean to...that is, I thought you were sleeping or I wouldn't have—"

"I've been up for an hour. Come on in."

For that particular instant, she couldn't seem to come or go. His chin was dipped in shaving foam and he had a razor in his hand. He wasn't wearing enough clothes, just jeans that slung dangerously low over his hips. The whole bathroom was warm with him. His hair was still damp from a shower, and the sun filtered through the droplets of water on his chest hair. For a fleeting moment, all she could think of was that she'd touched that chest hair, tasted it, smelled it, but she'd never seen it. She knew Mike naked by night, not by day.

"I'll be out of here in a few minutes, but feel free...." He motioned to the door inside the bathroom marked Ladies.

She'd use the room marked Ladies while he was three feet away when she was a white-haired senile old lady. "I...that wasn't the problem."

"No?" The razor glided over his chin; his eyes glinted at her from the mirror. "Did you sleep well?"

"Wonderfully." Which was partly true. She must have slept some of the night; she just couldn't remember when. She should have remembered from before that the madam's room wasn't conducive to sleeping.

"Come on. There's plenty of space for two. You're not shy around me, are you?" He moved over, which was unnecessary. There *was* plenty of room for two to do their morning ablutions. If the two were lovers, or past lovers.

The etiquette of past lovers wasn't Maggie's specialty. The night had not gone smoothly. She'd spent a lot of hours well aware that Mike was prepared to start where they'd left off, that she wouldn't have had to fight him if she'd crossed the hall again. Most men were hardly immune to a lady who threw it away free and clear, now were they?

"Thanks, but no," she said wryly to his offer of sharing the sink. "I'll use the downstairs bathroom. I just came in here because..."

"Hmmm?" Those dark eyes were picking up humor like radar spots a speeder.

"Because I needed to borrow something, if you wouldn't mind. I seemed to have forgotten to pack a towel."

"You didn't pack a lot of things this time, Maggie." He drew the thick velour towel from the rack and draped it over her arms. The towel was still warm from his skin, still faintly damp. It smelled exactly like him. "What else?"

"Washcloth?"

His eyes were dancing now. "What else?"

"Toothpaste and soap," she said crossly.

"My Maggie not prepared?" He tch-tched, stacking the toilet items on top of the towel. "Did you remember a toothbrush?"

"Yes!"

Downstairs in the small bathroom off the kitchen, she used his soap, his toothpaste, his towel. In the doing she felt like Mike had effectively stamped her his.

She whisked on mascara, a little lip gloss, blush. If makeup were a woman's armor, it struck her as chintzy protection. My Maggie not prepared? My Maggie. *My Maggie.* How dare he call her his Maggie?

When she walked back out to the kitchen, Mike was pouring two cups of coffee. His gaze frisked her more intimately than a cop looking for contraband. "You left your hair down," he said approvingly.

She felt abruptly exhausted. If he'd said one word, if he'd directly asked her to go to bed, if he'd so much as laid a finger on her, she would have known what to do. In fact, she'd had her lines prepared in Philadelphia, all about friends and honesty and the brisk moment of insanity that had overtaken her last February.

Instead, he just kept making her feel ... warm, welcomed in his life, wanted. He did it with his eyes and he'd done it with the flowers and the pounds of butterscotch; he did it by noticing that she'd left her hair down. None of it had to mean he loved her and Maggie was far too wary to let herself believe in that fantasy again, but a direct assault she would have known how to fight. Mike, she was discovering, was a sniper.

"Ready to go see Elsa?" he asked lightly.

"Elsa?"

"Elsa Grogan. The lady I told you we were going to visit this morning. She's our retired ... um ... lady of the night." Mike's grin was wicked when he caught the expression on Maggie's face. "You didn't realize what I meant when I said she worked for our grandfathers?"

"I—no." Maggie brought the steaming cup to her lips, and then back down again. "Mike, if she ... I mean she must be past eighty—"

"Well past," Mike agreed.

Maggie parted her lips to object. The only sensible choice she could possibly make this morning was to insist on seeing a real estate agent. The faster the place was sold, the faster she was completely away from here, the safer she was going to be.

Only the image of an eighty-year-old retired madam was rather irresistible.

The apartment was located in an old, established Indianapolis neighborhood. Inside, the furnishings were in a muted rose. Family photographs crowded every table and the place was populated with cats.

Elsa Grogan was eighty if a day. Curly wisps of white hair framed a tiny face with more lines than a wrinkled apple, and her blue eyes were full of laughter. Dressed in a pastel print dress, she served both of her visitors peppermint tea.

"Yes, lass, I worked for both your grandfathers, and I loved every minute of it. You two are too young to understand what the Depression did to people. Jobs disappeared; families went hungry; reality was gray and the future without a promise. You can't live day after day without laughter—just pet Pittsburg, sweetheart. He won't leave you alone until you do."

Maggie wasn't sure what she'd expected, but it wasn't peppermint tea, an angora cat trying to drape himself around her neck, and a little old lady who talked about her past affairs in such luxurious detail.

"My room was number nine," Elsa said with a frank chuckle.

Lord, Maggie thought. The red-white-and-blue one.

"It wasn't what you think...or maybe it was. Really, it was a question of geography. During prohibition times, if you wanted to transport liquor from the French Lick to Chicago, you used the river. Simple logistics. The law patrolled the roads; there was no way they could effectively control traffic on the river at night. Naturally enough, speakeasies popped up all along the water route. Your grandparents' place was simply one of those, and the thing was—people sometimes had to come quite a distance. You had to be able to offer them a place to stay overnight. That's all your grandparents had in mind with the rooms upstairs. There was just an occasion or two when the girls used the rooms a little differently." Dancing blue eyes pounced on Maggie. "Would you care for more peppermint tea?"

Mike made a small sound in his throat.

Maggie gently jabbed him in the ribs with her elbow. Damn the man. He'd flopped next to her on the horsehair sofa the minute they'd walked in. His eyes had been brimful of wicked laughter ever since. It was tough reconciling an offer for peppermint tea with images of madams, but Maggie was trying to concentrate. "No, thank you, Mrs. Grogan. You were going to tell us what happened after our grandfathers left the place."

"Yes, well...most of the places folded on the river once the liquor ban was repealed. Why should people come the distance when they could get a bottle of wine at their corner liquor store again? Of course, some of the other places simply converted into respectable bars, but I gather your grandfathers had their own interests in other parts of the country. They left an old man in charge of the place back then, just let him live there for a few years. Harry was his name, and he's dead now, but he's the one who told me that Dillinger hid out there three or four times.''

The lady had an hourful of stories about Dillinger, all of which led up to her firm conviction that there was bank money stashed in one of his hideouts and that the Ianelli-Flannery ''Willows'' was as good a place as any to start looking.

''But the man who was there, that 'Harry,' must have looked,'' Maggie objected. ''And our grandfathers—if they'd heard the stories, they could have come back and looked, too. For that matter, the government—''

''Sweetheart,'' Elsa said patiently, ''*everyone* looked. The point is that hundreds of thousands of dollars in gold bullion were never recovered, and that this is the area where Dillinger had to have hidden it.'' She paused. ''Did I tell you about Lorena? She's the one who stayed in that powder-blue room off the river....''

Mike made another small humorous sound in his throat as Elsa began another of her more personal anecdotes. And then, like a surprise, Maggie suddenly felt his fingers, slowly, unobtrusively sifting through her hair. His one arm was stretched on top of the couch back, making it easy for those fingers of his to touch her.

Maggie, still listening to Mrs. Grogan, heard another half dozen stories about a house filled with women in silks with fringe and ropes of pearls, and good-looking dangerous men who flaunted a life of risk in a daredevil way. Forbidden pleasures and treasure, she couldn't seem to get away from them any more than she could escape the lazy lethargic fingers at her nape. His thumb gently rubbed the corded muscle at the back of her neck. Like the cat named Pittsburg in her lap, she wanted to purr and arch her throat for the sensual touch.

Instead, she arched to her feet at the soonest possible moment. "I can't thank you enough for being willing to talk to us, Mrs. Grogan. We didn't mean to take up your entire morning."

In the car, while Mike started the engine, Maggie said darkly, "At least my grandfather wasn't married when he knew her."

Mike burst out laughing.

"Doesn't sound to me like your grandfather was much of a saint either, Ianelli. I don't know what you think you're laughing about."

"I wasn't laughing at you. I was just picturing what Elsa looked like in a flapper dress."

"You heard her! The red-white-and-blue room. Lord, the craziest color scheme in the whole darn house." But Maggie was starting to chuckle too. "I kept expecting her to whip out a cigarette, wink at me, and say 'we've come a long way, baby.'"

"She wasn't exactly the baking cookies kind of grandma, now was she?" Mike slowed the car and drove it onto the shoulder of the road.

She cocked a brow at him in surprise. "What's wrong?"

"Nothing's wrong. It's just decision time. A turn to the right would eventually lead us to the real estate office. I told you I'd handle that and I can, but if you're absolutely sure that's what you want we can start the business right now. Or," he motioned, "straight ahead will sooner or later end us up home, and treasure hunting. Your choice."

"You know darn well what my choice is," Maggie said testily.

"Do I?"

"Shut up and drive, Ianelli. But don't think for a minute I believed one silly word of that woman's stories."

"Of course you didn't," Mike agreed blandly.

Eight

Four hours later Maggie was on her knees in the lavender bedroom, running her hands inch by inch over the floorboards. "I'm still going up the dumb waiter after we get through searching the floors," Maggie insisted.

"When hell freezes over," Mike agreed.

"You said yourself the rope was as good as new. There's plenty of room for a person to crouch inside—"

"No."

"All you'd have to do was pull me up; I could check out all those inside walls."

"That's probably where the bats are nesting, Flannery."

Maggie sat back on her heels and rubbed at the dust smudge on her nose. "That's what you said when I wanted to check out the hole in the attic. Look, Michael. You seem to think all you have to do is mention bats and I'll—"

"Turn green? You do. It's very effective." Mike shot her an amused glance. After nearly four hours of turning the house upside down for treasure, Maggie's jeans were dusty, her sweater disheveled, and her hair was flying every which way. Maggie didn't do anything half throttle.

They'd found an empty safe, copper casings in two other bedrooms' floorboards, and a lot of dust from attic to basement. Mike hadn't expected to find treasure but then he wasn't treasure hunting.

He was being with Maggie.

A canvas shoe nudged his calf. "You're not giving up already?" she scolded.

"Of course not." His hands skimmed the floor. His eyes watched Maggie's fanny weave back and forth as she continued to test for loose floorboards. She had such a nice fanny. Trim, low-hipped, curved exactly right. Her eyes suddenly whipped in his direction, all suspicion. He met her look squarely, all innocence. "I'm looking," he insisted in an injured tone, and paused. "Maggie?"

"Hmmm?"

The last thing he wanted to do was break her good mood, but unfortunately she was returning to Philadelphia in less than twenty four hours unless he did something. "I've been thinking. About who might want to buy a place like this."

"Yes?" Her hands kept moving.

"The fact is that it's just too big a place to keep up for your average individual home owner. Now, a condominium developer might be interested, particularly because there's river property. Of course they'd have to tear down the house."

A cold clot formed in the pit of her stomach.

"Realistically, my bet is that even if an individual could afford to keep the house, he'd want to completely tear up the insides. Lower the ceilings, partition the rooms, tear out the old chandeliers." He hesitated. "Rip out the kitchen. It'd be a shame to lose the character of the place, but energy costs being what they are—"

"The right person could make it energy efficient without destroying the place," Maggie said stiffly. Horrible images darted through her mind, of chrome kitchens and fake paneling and fluorescent lighting.

"The right person, yes." He trailed her from the lavender room across the hall to the scarlet one. Once inside, he leaned back against the wall. "The right person," he continued lazily, "might be able to maintain the place as it is, if she ran a self-supporting business out of it. The kind of seminar business you suggested, for instance. It's an ideal location to draw executives from surrounding industry—"

Green eyes whirled on him. Did he have to keep gnawing at the sore? The dream that had taken hold of her two months ago was hard enough to let go of. "That was a good pipe dream, Ianelli, nothing more."

"No?"

"No. A woman has to be practical. Realistic."

"And you've decided the idea is totally unrealistic?"

"Yes," she confirmed, and lowered her eyes. "For one thing, I have a good job in Philadelphia."

"So you told me. Assistant Product Manager, wasn't that it? So you're totally attached to your job?"

"Totally."

"You mentioned your boss one time," Mike probed. "Sounded like he was a good man to work for."

"He is." Maggie glared at him. How'd he managed to find another sore point? Her boss was terrific; he'd taught her everything he knew and then some. Absolutely the only problem with Frank was that he was in his early thirties, which meant her chances of promotion in the small company were dependent on his retiring thirty years from now. "Regardless, my job isn't the only issue," she said firmly.

"No?"

"No." Her hands skimmed the floorboards. This was her chance to impress him with how realistic and sensible she really was, to show him she was nothing like the frivolous dreamer he'd met in February. "For one thing, there's nothing to say I could make a go of it. I may have a business background but zillions of people have business backgrounds. My ties are all in

Philadelphia. It would take more than a season to build a business like that up, and a heck of a lot of work and capital to get this whole place in shape. The key word is capital, and I can't imagine anyone willing to float a fortune in capital for a pipe dream.''

"There's a man named Allen Frisk. A banker in town. I checked with him several weeks ago, green eyes. He'll talk capital with you. I don't know how he feels about pipe dreams, but he seems to think you have an excellent idea.''

Suddenly Maggie couldn't be busier. It gave her immense satisfaction to examine every floorboard. Thoughts skidded through her mind. She felt wonder that Mike had done that for her; horror that he'd done that for her.

She desperately wanted the house. For years she'd wanted the dream that this place represented to her, and for two months she'd planned and replanned how she could successfully make a go of a business here. But that wasn't the point. The whole issue had become irreparably tangled with her feelings for Mike. Yes, she wanted to start the darned business, but how could she possibly stay in this house without thinking of him?

And all day, the whole damned day, she'd had fun with him. She'd never meant to get caught up in this silly business of treasure hunting, never considered how lethally dangerous being with Mike again could be. She'd let down her guard because she hadn't been able to help it. She only had Mike and her dream of keeping the house for a few short hours. There seemed no harm in just enjoying his company and stocking up memories for cold winter nights. She just wanted to remember what his laughter sounded like. How could there be any harm in that?

Only there was harm, she thought fleetingly. She was in love with the man, and being anywhere near him promoted dangerous fantasies about being loved back. Ianelli was kind. He was also willing to share a bed. That wasn't love. It was a shared inheritance that made a temporary relationship convenient, and this time she was determined to be realistic.

"Flannery, I'm not going to wait forever."

She rocked back on her heels again. "For what?"

"Honesty." His dark eyes bore into hers, demanding, not asking.

Maggie felt painfully helpless. Honesty—now there was the steel shaft of the knife blade. Mike had already been honest with her. They'd shared a couple of nights that he'd admitted were special for him. As long as she didn't call it love.

Her eyes dropped beneath his steady stare.

"Maggie—"

"I'm thinking, I'm thinking." And her hands were moving restlessly. Suddenly they stopped. Beneath her fingers, she'd discovered a loose floorboard, and then another. "Ianelli!" He was beside her in seconds, but her voice was still a triumphant roar.

"Now don't get your hopes up. It's just going to be another empty cavity."

"Who cares?"

"Get your fingers out of the way. Let me use the crowbar."

"I can do it. It's just—ouch!" She brought up the pinched finger and shook it.

Moments before, he'd been tempted to shake her. He was still tempted, now for different reasons. "Let's see the finger."

"Forget me. Pull up the darn boards!"

The two-foot cavity had been insulated with copper, like the other ones they'd discovered. Only this one wasn't empty. Five minutes later, Mike handed Maggie the first of their booty. Five minutes after that, there were a dozen green bottles of champagne lined under the window in the late-afternoon's sunlight.

Both were totally silent, staring at the bottles. Then at each other. "So? Who needs gold bullion?" Maggie said blithely.

Mike's tone was wry. "A case of 1923 Rothschild is probably better than gold bullion."

"If that's a small hint that they're too valuable to open, tough petunias to you, Ianelli. Maybe—*maybe*—I can wait long enough for one bottle to be properly chilled." She frowned. "I suppose they're all ruined. All that exposure to heat and cold through the years?"

He shrugged. "The cavity was well insulated, and each bottle was wrapped up pretty well. Don't forget our grandfathers must have been prepared to hide their liquor against raids. They wouldn't have risked it being ruined in the meantime."

"Still..."

"Another hint that we'd better open one and see?" With a broad grin, Mike lurched to his feet, and reached down a hand for Maggie. "Are you dying more of curiosity or thirst, Flannery—as if I didn't know?"

"Both." Her palm disappeared willingly in his, but when she was standing and made to automatically pull away, he didn't release her hand.

"We'll toast our treasure first," he said lightly.

She thought his hold was accidental, until his fingers suddenly tightened on hers. And until she looked up. His mouth was suddenly a breath away. Pale sunlight slanted on his dark hair, on his temples and the slash of his cheekbones. She could feel his palm against hers, warm and hard.

Sensual vibrations invaded the still room. The short silence seemed to overflow with emotions she'd been trying so hard to deny. All day, laughter had come so easily. All day, simply being with him had made her high. It wasn't enough, she knew that. "Mike," she said softly, and stopped. There wasn't anything to say.

"We're going to toast your treasure first," he repeated firmly, "and then—right after you admit you want to give up this house like you want to give up your right arm—we're going to toast your starting a new business."

"Yes."

He'd never expected her immediate acquiescence.

Neither had Maggie. The damn word had popped out from nowhere.

* * *

"You're not going to change your mind?"

"If you come back in another life, it's going to be as a badger. No, I'm not going to change my mind."

"You're sure?"

"Of course I'm not sure. This is insane." Maggie's eyes were closed. A serious note crept into her voice in spite of herself. "The very soonest I could come up with a proposal for the bank would be three weeks. Three months would be more logical. I need realistic costs on paper of what it would take to fix the place up and start it running. The bank will want proof that I have the ability to draw in business, which means time to contact companies and see if I can interest them in this location..."

Mike grinned. It was obvious that Maggie had spent ample time thinking the project through, long before their discussion. "You'll have it open by September."

"There is no possible way to have it open by September," she said with a sigh. Once Ianelli got hold of a cause, there was clearly no stopping him. Talking was useless.

"Once you get your costs together, I'll do the financial report for you. All you have to do is decide what you need done in the place..."

"Ianelli?"

"What?"

"If I swear to the high heavens that I'm even half as excited about this project as you are, that I'm not going to let it go, that as of Monday morning I'm giving my notice on the best-paid job I've ever had, could we drop this for a minute and a half?"

Silence. "I was pushing a little?" he asked delicately.

"In your last life you were a steamroller. Where is my bottle?"

"Ah, my big drinker's thirsty again."

She let the "my" pass. For the next few minutes she let a lot of things pass. Business talk just didn't belong here. For a time, quiet enveloped them both.

More than an hour before, they'd both agreed that the river was the only possible spot to celebrate treasures. Mike had brought the blanket and a jar of nuts. Maggie'd brought the champagne. They were at the river bank now, both reclined, facing the sky.

The sun was pure white on the water. Birds were too lazy to come out this late in the day, but the squirrels couldn't control their curiosity—mostly because Mike kept throwing them nuts. The trees threw long, sun-dappled shadows that shifted in the faintest sylvan breeze. Conceivably there'd been another spring afternoon like this one, but Maggie didn't believe it. She moved only to reach for the champagne.

Mike had one eye cocked open, watching her take a sip. Every time she'd taken a drink, she'd watched his lips form a distinctly male grin.

"You know, the best part about this—" she tapped the half empty bottle "—isn't the taste, or any nonsense about the 'bouquet of the wine,' or even the bubbles."

"Rothschild Vineyards will be depressed to hear you say that. Assuming they're still in business." Mike leaned up on an elbow. "I give up. What's the best part?"

"Drinking in the middle of the afternoon, and out of the bottle yet. I mean seriously now—how degenerate can you get?"

"I can't imagine how you could go farther downhill," Mike agreed gravely.

"You're equally depraved, you know."

"But then, I already knew I couldn't go farther downhill. Pass the bottle, green eyes."

"You're welcome to it. Enough is enough."

"So much," Mike said wryly, "for depraved."

Maggie tried to work up enough energy to kick him, but the somnolent blend of champagne and sunlight had gradually affected her muscles. Actually, both bones and muscles appeared to have melted in such a position that her legs were stretched out, her arms were forming a pillow behind her head, and her eyes were permanently at half-mast. Efforts to change this position failed. Efforts to think failed. The smells of river and grass and spring were just too dazzling.

Mike's eyes suddenly appeared directly in front of her own, not an illogical happening since he was lying right next to her. "You couldn't have had more than the equivalent of one glass of champagne, you know. It's like watching a freight train turn into a marshmallow. All that energy seriously disappears with a few sips of champagne?"

"I resent—a lot—being called a freight train." Her eyes narrowed on his; she tried for a scowl. "Last February, you didn't tease like this."

"No?"

"It's not an improvement in character, Ianelli."

"No?"

The man exhausted her. She closed her eyes again, savoring the difference in Mike between last February and now. Months ago he'd been broody. He'd worn pride like a mask and loneliness had radiated from him. Now he was annoyingly cocky, his sick sense of humor repeatedly surfaced, and nothing escaped his roving black eyes. She was glad for him. She told herself over and over that whatever the trouble in his life had been, it wasn't her business...but she was still glad for him.

She was less happy for herself. The original F. Michael Ianelli had appealed to every feminine gene, cell and atom in her body. The new version of Ianelli was doubly dangerous to her peace of mind. She'd meant to spend the day in a real estate office not treasure hunting. She'd never meant to agree to keeping the house, and she certainly had no idea what she was doing lying on a blanket near the river next to dynamite. Everything that had gone wrong was his fault.

The damn man kept managing to give her the impression he wanted to be with her. She wasn't kidding herself that it was forever. While she'd known from the beginning she wasn't the kind of woman to appeal long-term to a man like Mike she also knew she couldn't live with another short affair, which effectively left her in limbo.

At the moment, limbo was as heady as the taste of champagne. In an hour or two, she'd do some kind of terrible penance for letting herself fantasize again. Right now she wouldn't worry about it.

"If you're not totally asleep, I'd like to tell you something," Mike said idly.

"I'm listening," she murmured.

But he was silent for a long moment. Her eyes fluttered open and she turned her head. Mike was just lying there, a blade of grass between his teeth and his hands behind his head. He could have looked lazier, but it would have been hard.

When he suddenly twisted his head, though, that aura of laziness was instantly gone. Shadows screened the expression in his eyes, but she could sense the old broodiness. "Maybe," he said quietly, "you'd better have a little more champagne before you hear this."

Maggie didn't need any more champagne. "What's wrong?" she said instantly.

"Nothing." Everything. He'd set up the day, from the visit with Elsa Grogan to treasure hunting to champagne by a sleepy river. He'd set up the day to appeal to the dreamer in Maggie, and it seemed to be working. Only Mike was all too aware that was never what he'd wanted at all. She seemed content with the way things were, content to dismiss him as a stranger who passed occasionally through her life. He was all too conscious that she never wanted more than the fantasy.

He pushed himself up to a sitting position and balanced back against the gnarled trunk of an old hickory. "You're the only woman I ever met in my life who didn't pry," he said idly.

She tried to smile and then gave up trying. Wrapping her arms around her knees, she worried about whatever he was finding so hard to say. "From the time I first met you, you made it pretty clear you wanted to keep your privacy," she said quietly.

"When I first met you, that was how I felt," he admitted. "But that had nothing to do with you personally, Maggie."

"It was your business," she assured him.

Because you don't want to know, love? But I'll be damned if I'm going to leave it at that. He found an old stick, and started peeling the bark from it. "Last June," he said finally, "I lost a job at a company by the name of Stuart-Spencer's. The reason they gave me was that the company was being reorganized, and my position no longer existed. That wasn't true." He faced her. "I was the chief financial officer for the company, and some forty thousand dollars had been juggled out of the till. Only three people had access to that money—the president, vice-president, and myself."

"Lord, Mike . . ."

"I knew exactly where those funds were," he clipped out, which effectively put a stricken look in her eyes. *It's a long bump down to reality, isn't it, Maggie? I'm no one's fantasy lover, and never was.* "I knew where the money was, but I didn't know how that would affect my life from that point on. I applied for job after job, couldn't get a soul to give me an interview. Finally I cornered a man I'd worked with before and he admitted that Stuart-Spencer's had been labeling me a thief. He made it more than clear that I didn't have a prayer of finding a position in finance anywhere in the hemisphere."

"Bastards." Maggie said. An ache squeezed her heart, so fast. Mike valued honesty like he valued air. A slur that monumental to his integrity must have killed him. "You were set up."

He shook his head. "You don't know that."

"Ianelli, don't be an ass! Of course I know that!" She got on her knees, facing him like a tigress daring a passerby to look twice at her cub. "That was what was bothering you last February, wasn't it?"

He didn't answer that. "A president and vice-president are hardly going to steal from their own company, now are they? Believe me, every shred of evidence was against me, is against me—"

"If you're trying to convince me you're a thief, you can forget it."

"I'm *trying* to make you see this realistically."

"I am," she said fiercely.

"Maggie..." He just shook his head. Relief flooded through him like a sigh. Maggie being Maggie, perhaps he should have guessed she'd automatically believe in him. The lady was a long way from a cynical realist. He felt relief that she hadn't shown even a moment of doubt. Ducking his head, he systematically started shedding bark from the stick again.

"I went to the labor board and an attorney. There are laws against blackballing a man's references without proof. On paper, though, there was nothing but 'position terminated.' References were given over the telephone, but no one was willing to stand up in court and admit what was being said to them. Unless specific charges were filed against me, I had nothing to fight back with."

He would have kept on talking—he wanted to keep on talking. Except that Maggie was suddenly all over him. His half-peeled stick was hurled toward the river. She dropped onto his lap as if she expected to be welcomed. Her arms went around his neck as if they would lock there. "Damn you for not telling me this before," she said furiously. "I've never met such a fool, Ianelli. Never. I swear I could..."

Nine

———

She was so angry, Mike realized. There was so much he needed to put into words—exactly why he hadn't called her, why he hadn't felt he had the right to when he was without a job. And he wanted to find some way to make her express her feelings, force her to admit that that long-ago weekend had been more than fantasies and loneliness and need for both of them. He wanted to talk to Maggie about honesty, but she'd stopped listening. Her eyes were the color of hot jade and her face white.

His lips just touched hers in a beguiling kiss meant to soothe and quiet her anger. His lips touched, then withdrew. Touched, then withdrew. He felt warm, then cold. Alive, then not. For all those lonely months, he'd defined life in terms of pride and work and a man's integrity. He was wrong. The touch of Maggie was life.

The grass rushed up to cushion Maggie's back. The sky tilted to make a backdrop for Mike's raven hair, his dark eyes. He really deserved a lecture about not taking on things alone, about having a little faith that other people just might have always been on his side, but his kisses sapped anger, energy, sweetness from her. She was distracted by the weight of the man and by her own need to obliterate the loneliness of the past few months. By loving him, and wanting to surround him with that love. Left, was a heady sensation of urgency that might have either come from Mike or her. It didn't matter where.

It was cool in the shade, hot in the sun. They rolled like tumbleweeds, Maggie holding on. First, the rush of the river filled her ears, then she noticed the intense quiet of a late afternoon. Length to length, she felt the beat of his heart, the unyielding sinew of his thighs. Denim scraped against denim. He pushed up her sweater; she tugged at his shirt; and still he kissed her.

His skin was golden warm, and the moment she touched him his lips dragged like a weight over hers. She could taste his hunger. She could feel it, smell it. He wanted to be touched by her, now. She had a thousand images in her head of the kind of lover Mike normally wanted. None of them were flat-chested; none of them were redheads with a spray of freckles on their nose.

He kissed that spray of freckles. He pushed past a tangle of sweater and bra straps and found an oversensitive nubbin. He lavishly tongued that nipple before searching out its mate. Against her thigh, she could feel the hard pulse of man against her, and a shiver rocked her from her toes to her crown.

All her life she'd aroused men to little more than polite kisses. With Mike it was so different. She was so different. For the ten thousand reasons she knew it was wrong to have fallen in love with him, she knew this was right. He would leave her. She would simply have to live with that again. For months, she'd hungered for the man who knew the other Maggie. The Maggie who wanted to be beautiful, passionate, and not good at all. The Maggie who could make a man forget that he was alone. The Maggie who wickedly reveled in the feel of bare cool grass beneath her back, and had no idea where her sweater was.

Her jeans also seemed to be missing. Mike stopped kissing long enough to look at her. His eyes dawdled over white satin skin, the frantic rise and fall of small perfect breasts, the jade glow in her eyes. The faintest color touched her skin when he looked; he smiled.

When she reached over to undo his jeans, he stopped smiling. Her fingers had magic. She skimmed his jeans down, inch by inch, deliberately slow. Her palms grazed the wiry hair on his thighs, rubbed against the natural grain.

When he reached for her, she whisked just beyond the grasp of his hands. She was suddenly standing, tugging the rest of his jeans off by the hems. Only he didn't trust the odd mischievous glint in her eyes.

"Maggie—"

She'd seen his smile. An arrogant smile. A very sure-of-himself, confident, intimate lover's smile. It was distinctly *not* the smile of a man for his favorite niece.

"Come back here," he roared.

"Catch me," she whispered back. Stark naked, she ran, arms outflung. There were ninety acres to run through in privacy, through sunlight and shadows, inviting his laughter, teasing him with hers. Loving was a celebration. She wanted to be sure he knew. Life was too impossibly rich not to celebrate Mike...and Maggie. And this kind of treasure.

When he caught up with her, she was breathless and laughing, more when he raised her sky-high as if she weighed no more than a cotton puff. But when he lowered her back down, he lowered her against the length of him. He was hard exactly where she was soft. Chest and thigh nuzzled against chest and thigh, all bare. Breeze-cooled skin turned warm, then hot.

He lowered her to a carpet of grass and clover. "You're like wind. Like song, Maggie," he whispered.

When he went inside her, she wrapped legs, arms, soul around him. There was a flowering white dogwood near by, scenting the air. So sweet. Mike's taking her took on that wild sweetness. She felt the tiny flutter of wings inside her. And then soared.

* * *

Thunder grumbled in the distance as Maggie grabbed her briefcase and purse and raced for the veranda steps. Where early April had been constantly warm and sunny, the end of May was proving volatile. Lightning slashed. She took a fleeting glance just before ducking into the house. She loved a storm particularly when safe inside.

Dropping her burdens on the couch, she tugged off her pale yellow suit jacket and left it on a chair. Her gaze whisked around the room—it still held nothing more than two threadbare couches and a fireplace. Even though she'd moved from Philadelphia several weeks ago, she'd done very little with the house but lavish the downstairs walls with a fresh coat of antique white paint. Serious decorating changes were dependent on her just-concluded visit to the bank.

Her mind was full of construction estimates, liability clauses, Indiana licensing laws, and financial statements. Not surprisingly, there was an annoying pounding in her ears, but as it happened, she had no headache.

She trailed the pounding sound to the kitchen doorway and shook her head. Although the top half of his body was buried under the sink, Ned Whistler's stubby legs and scratched work boots were unmistakable. A smattering of tools was scattered beside him. From the sounds of four-letter words echoing from under the sink, she gathered rather quickly that the plumbing wasn't behaving, and crouched down.

"You were *not* supposed to come in today," she scolded.

"You're back." Ned pushed out from under the sink, his wizened features contorted in a grimace until he caught a look at her. Somewhere between fifty and a hundred and ten—Maggie had never figured out his age—Ned had squinty blue eyes, a respectable pot belly, a habit of hitching up his trousers, and a general scowl intended to scare off the world.

"Can I help?" she asked gently.

The scowl never worked well with Maggie, mostly because he couldn't seem to hold on to it when she was around. His eyes softened now, looking her over. The pale yellow skirt matched a pair of yellow pumps, and her white silk blouse was tied with a blue-and-yellow scarf. For once, her hair was almost elegantly behaving. "Don't you get anywhere near this mess," he scolded.

Ignoring him, she perched down on her haunches, trying to peer in. "What's wrong?"

"What's wrong is that I want to put a new pipe tee in there so I can divert the water flow to a bathroom on the other side. Only the confounded old pipes don't want to match up with the confounded new ones."

"Ah," Maggie said knowledgeably. "Are we talking a brute-strength or a technology-type problem here?"

"We're talking dadblame copper-pipe-type problems."

"We're also talking total shock, since this is the first I've heard of a bathroom on the other side. Plus, Mr.

Whistler, you know darn well I can't afford you to come in every day—"

"It's Mr. Ianelli paying the wages and Mr. Ianelli's sayin' you need another bathroom, and I told you before to call me Ned."

Maggie's lips tightened. A battle had been building over money for weeks between her and Mike. In a sense, she was looking forward to it. Compressed emotions could only be packed in so long before they threatened to explode, and money was a reasonably safe subject to explode over. But in the meantime, Mr. Whistler was back under the sink, and she heard the unmistakable sound of bare skull meeting unyielding metal. A flat epitaph followed, referring to the parentage of the world in general.

Maggie ducked down again. "Maybe I can help. I've fixed a leaky faucet in my time—"

"You git out of here altogether. You're going to get yourself all dirty...."

"If I hold this for you—"

"You're not holding nothing."

"This one, then—"

"Never seen no woman as stubborn as you are," Ned Whistler said disgustedly. "And this is what I need you to hold on to. Just keep it in place for me for two whole minutes. This whole thing'll be done then."

A half hour later Ned was wiping his hands on a rag. A cup of some sissy-type tea was waiting for him on the counter. If he'd had his choice, he would have preferred a shot of hooch, but Maggie persisted in thinking he was a nice old man.

"Fixed the riding mower this morning and tackled those screens," he told her gruffly. "Tomorrow I figure I'll get into the pantry, work on those shelves. And you're getting new lighting in here. I know what you said." He motioned to the greenery over the window that Maggie hadn't been able to resist putting up, then the blue-and-white curtains and the hanging copper pots. "I know you ain't ready to do the rest of the kitchen, and I know you're all hung up on doing it old-fashioned. God knows why. Anyway, good lighting ain't gonna cost you any big fortune. You still gotta be able to see to cook and I'm putting it in, so that's that."

They were arguing lighting when Maggie's skin felt suddenly, oddly warm. She turned to find Mike in the doorway. His hands were in the pockets of his gray suit, and his white starched shirt was a startling contrast to the windblown hair that carelessly fell on his forehead, colored wet-raven from raindrops.

She steeled herself against feeling any sexual reaction as she'd been trying to do for weeks. It didn't work. His mouth was against her...that dry grin of his; he'd heard the argument between her and Whistler before. And she saw the impatient question in his eyes, but she also saw something else. It's been two nights since I've had you in bed, Maggie.

She was angry with Mike about money and mad at herself, for allowing a relationship to continue that she simply couldn't live with. Her lips parted to release an infinitely cautious greeting. Instead, she said the softest, "Hi."

"Hi, back."

Mr. Whistler raised his eyes to the ceiling, and smothering a grin, gathered up his tools. "I'm leaving. See you in the morning." He added slyly, "To do the lighting."

"Okay," Maggie said vaguely, and then frowned at his short bark of a laugh. A moment later he was gone.

She looked to find Mike bending into the open refrigerator, moving aside lettuce and cheese to reach a beer. He knew exactly where it was, and that he could count on his favorite brand being stocked.

"You look tired," Maggie remarked gently. "Saxton put you through his paces again?"

Saxton was a safe subject, and Maggie honestly loved hearing stories about his boss. One of the first nights she'd moved there, Mike had taken her to dinner to meet him. George was a combination ogre, bully, slave driver, and peddler. The two men shot challenges off each other like Ping-Pong balls. They'd paused between volleys only to make sure she was fed, watered, and happy. Maggie had been happy. Mike had told Saxton frankly that he intended to run his company; Saxton had flared up that he dared him to try. Saxton was the kind of man who frightened Maggie but Mike treated him like an arrogant child who needed taming. Both men radiated the same aura of integrity. Beating out the rest of the world was only a kick if you got all the credit for doing it fair and square.

"He thinks he wants me to come with him to St. Paul next week for three days. Found some derelict little company he wants to pick up—and no, I don't want to talk business. At least not my business."

Mike popped the lid on the beer can, took a long drink, and indulged himself in a long look at Maggie. Her pale yellow skirt had a good sized smudge on it. Under artificial light her hair looked like a blend of brown sugar and copper. A strand had loosened to curl around her cheek. Perfection only lasted so long around Maggie. She was capable of a certain kind of beauty when everything was arranged just so. He absolutely hated it when she was arranged just so…and when her eyes shied from his, like they were doing now.

"You're going to go? To St. Paul?"

"Probably." He thought, it'll be fine again once you seduce her. Maggie melted like butter in bed. He already knew that she loved the lover and he realized that they couldn't keep on like this forever. He'd had high hopes that working closely together these last two months would show her they had something real and tangible together. "Flannery?"

Her head was ducked in the refrigerator, searching for the makings of dinner. "Hmmm?"

"Are you going to keep me in suspense forever? What happened?"

"Well," Maggie set carrots on the counter, and opened the drawer for a peeler. "Mr. Frisk looked over all the plans. He felt the construction estimates were low. That I needed a better contract for liability—"

"Maggie!"

"He seemed astonished that I'd managed to get so many groups to even tentatively commit to coming here. Frankly, I was a little insulted. Obviously, I had to have a fairly good idea I could make a go of the place or I would have had nothing to discuss with him. That Dorothy Langley I told you about—she's the one who really helped, because she normally gives twelve seminars in a year to small groups, and this place was exactly what she—"

Extremely firm hands closed on her shoulders. Still carrying a carrot and peeler she was whirled around, and her chin tilted up to face a volatile pair of black eyes. Lots of good intentions were somehow jettisoned. She'd never intended to keep him in suspense, anyway, but the goal had been trying to keep the conversation businesslike. "I got the money," she said meekly.

"All of it?"

"All of it. And not a year's operating loan, but eighteen months." A huge grin formed on her lips in spite of herself. "Of course, I had to seduce him right there in front of all the tellers for that extra six months—"

"Don't fib, Flannery. If you'd seduced him, he'd probably be paying you interest for the right to give you money." His gaze dawdled over the suppressed excitement in her eyes, the flush of color in her cheeks that came from the afternoon's victory. He knew she'd been terrified of that interview.

She cocked her head. "You think I'm that good?"

"Hush. If you think I'm going to stand here and tell you how beautiful you are and how damned enticing I find you in bed..." His lips pressed on hers, hard and sweet. He meant the kiss to simply celebrate her successful meeting at the bank, only banks were suddenly the last thing on his mind. Her mouth was first cool under his; her shoulders almost imperceptibly stiffened. Not for long. Maggie was too giving to withhold a response for long. "You're beautiful, little one." His finger traced her cheek. "Sexy. Smart. Desirable..."

She ignored the shiver threatening to overtake her. "Continue," Maggie coaxed mischievously. "This is fascinating."

A smile kissed a smile, but Mike was well aware she was fighting him. The quip wasn't like Maggie. She stepped back, a little too fast. Her lashes fluttered down to screen the expression in her eyes. "I've got a present for you," he announced abruptly. "But you have to go outside to see it."

"What is it?"

He grabbed her hand, and pausing only long enough to throw his raincoat over her shoulders, led her outside. Instead of the car he normally drove, there was a pickup parked in the drive. Rain was coming down slick and fast. He tugged the raincoat over her head. "And keep your eyes closed now," he ordered her.

She closed her eyes, and was led blindly to the pickup bed. She heard the creak when he pushed down the tailgate, then felt his hands on her hips as he nudged her forward another foot or two.

"Now open."

She opened her eyes and jerked his raincoat off her head. Rain tried to cloud her vision, but she could see clearly enough that the spotless pickup bed held paint. Thirty gallons of it.

Mike had considered giving her roses if her venture at the bank was successful. Except that paint would captivate Maggie as roses clearly wouldn't. She'd shied away every time he'd tried to honestly express his feelings to her. All she wanted to do was talk business except during the times they weren't talking at all.

Her palm touched her forehead, momentarily blocking her face. "Antique white, like the room we already did. I knew you liked that color," he said. "The two of us can tackle the rest of it, Maggie. Evenings and weekends—" When she raised brimming eyes to his, his own widened in alarm. "Lord. I didn't mean to make you cry."

She walked into his arms, ignoring the rain and the clap of thunder in the distance, ignoring every internal vow she'd made not to initiate touch. "I'm not crying. It's just you, Ianelli. I don't know when you bought this, but you must have been damn sure I'd be successful at the bank."

"Of course I was sure." Water was spattering in her hair, already matting her eyelashes. Her lips were wet. Mesmerized, he couldn't take his eyes off them. "You were going to knock him dead, I told you that on the phone this morning."

She shook her head. "I never believed it." She sighed. "I love the paint."

When he moved to kiss her, she abruptly pulled away. "There's so much to do," she wailed suddenly. "Painting everything. I've got to set up an office. The bedrooms upstairs—"

Mike's eyes seared on hers. "We can go upstairs right now and change clothes if you're in such a hurry to get started."

"After dinner..."

"After dinner then."

She made it through dinner, and she made it through changing into paint-spattered white jeans and a football jersey, and she made it through laughing while lugging the gallons in from Mike's borrowed pickup. They first argued, then agreed, that starting to paint the upstairs would involve less immediate mess for the rest of the house. She stayed cool and in control right up to the time they carried two paint containers to the red-white-and-blue bedroom upstairs.

That seemed to be the exact moment it occurred to Mike that it was the one bedroom they hadn't christened. Every other bed in the house had been, well, initiated.

She didn't have to succumb, of course. She didn't have to respond to his kisses or laugh at his nonsense about every bed in the house needing a private initiation by the two of them. She didn't have to let him pull off her jersey and jeans.

But she could no more have stopped responding to Ianelli than quit breathing. Mike wasn't nice, not this time. He wasn't in a sweet lazy mood but a dangerous one. His caresses claimed; his teeth nipped and teased; he spun a silken web around Maggie that sapped her of will and promised magic and demanded she match him, touch for touch. The mattress groaned in unison with the thunder outside; lightning slashed inside of her. She cried his name; it seemed what he wanted. It wasn't enough; he wanted more. And more...

A lifetime later, her cheek was curled to his shoulder in the darkness. Eyes closed, she listened to the rain battering against the windows. Her legs were still tangled with his, and her whole body felt limp, sated, tingling with the aftermath of their loving. Mike's palm kept smoothing over her skin in a touch that was tender and protective and soothing.

Only her heart kept beating, beating, beating, as if she were waiting for something. Waiting for him to realize she was only Maggie, waiting for him to leave her again?

For the past two months she'd let herself believe in fantasies again...the dream that she could have it all, that he loved her, that she had the power of a woman to hold him.

Only she didn't believe it. Reality was that Mike was a kind man, that he was helping her with the house and that in a few short weeks the house would be done. Reality was that she'd made herself shamelessly convenient for him, as if she were the kind of woman who could blithely give herself sexually without a thought to the future. And reality was discovering that she had too much pride to keep letting that go on.

From the first time they'd made love, Mike had never been less than honest with her. He'd told her then that his feelings didn't include love. A dozen times he'd tried to talk to her about honesty, warning her about illusions people had about love, and she'd cut him off every time. She already knew she was guilty of illusions. She'd tried to convince herself that she didn't care, that loving Mike for now was better than never loving him at all, but it wasn't working.

The cliff just kept getting higher, and Maggie couldn't stop waiting for the fall.

"Cold, little one?"

She turned her head. "No."

"You were shivering." He reached down for her jersey and tugged it over her head, then snuggled next to her with a smile. Her copper hair was all wispy. The neck of her jersey sagged at her throat, making her neck look impossibly vulnerable. Her smooth bare legs glided against his rough ones.

"Mike?" Her fingers combed the wiry hair on his chest.

"Hmmm?" She was tickling him; he pulled her hand around his neck. From there it seemed a natural extension to tickle her in return. He rubbed the graze of his beard in the hollow of her throat, savoring her softness. "We're not getting much painting done."

"No." She closed her eyes, feeling his smooth lips on her pulse. To never feel that kiss again? She couldn't face it. But smaller things, maybe she could manage to at least face the smaller things. Somehow she had to salvage a little pride, a little self-respect. "Could we talk?"

"Of course."

She took a breath. "Now that I've been to the bank, I've got operating funds."

"Yes." She was saying the obvious; he leaned back and cocked his brow questioningly.

"Which means that I'm in a position to pay you rent for your half of the house and property—"

"We've been over this." Suddenly every muscle in his body tensed. "I don't want rent, Maggie."

"It isn't right," she said carefully. "We both inherited this place, not just me. You've been pouring money into the house hand over fist. And the checks I gave you for my half of the expenses, Mike...I know you didn't cash last month's—"

"I earn an adequate salary. I don't need your money, and you're trying to get a new business on its feet. Contrary to what you seem to think, it won't kill you to accept a little help when you need it. Assuming—" he let out a harsh breath "—that we're even talking about money."

She raised up on her knees, pushed back her hair.

"Well? Maggie? Are you talking about money?"

She shook her head and wondered vaguely if her heart was going to cave in. His tone was cold and his eyes furious. He looked as approachable as stone.

"Money is part of it, but no...not all," she said haltingly. "I just can't keep letting you give me money to help me get this place on its feet. You never asked for this shared inheritance to begin with, nor should it be your financial problem because I'm the one who wants to keep the property—"

"I only wish money were what we were talking about. Spill it, Maggie."

She swallowed hard. "Please don't sound so angry."

"I'm not angry," he clipped out, and took a long look at her. With her arms wrapped around her legs and her face all white, she looked like a curled-up kitten waiting for a blow...and he knew darn well *he* was the one about to be hit, and hard. "Hell," he said wearily. "Do you think I couldn't guess this talk was coming? You want to talk about the two of us, isn't that what this is about?"

"Yes." For an instant, the words couldn't get past the lump in her throat, and then they spilled out like tumbling marbles. "Mike, I just want to be honest with you—you were the one who stressed honesty from the beginning. I know you don't believe that I really...cared about you at first. You said it was important that we both admit that we came together because of need, and not color all that up with words about love. I won't tell you I felt otherwise because I know you wouldn't believe that...so maybe I did reach out to you out of need when we first met, but that's changed—I've changed."

"Yes. You don't need me anymore, do you, honey?" Mike raised up slowly from the bed, and reached for his clothes. It didn't take him long to don jeans and a sweatshirt. "A few months ago, you thought you needed a lover—only the real world was bound to hit you sooner or later, little one. You were always stronger than you thought you were. You were always strong enough to reach out for what you wanted in your life, Maggie. And I always really knew you didn't need me."

"Mike…" Confused and upset, she shook her head bewilderedly. "That was never what I meant."

"Of course it is. Ships that passed in the night," he grated flatly. "You badly needed someone to believe in you for a short time, while you put your life back together. So did I need someone, Maggie, but our lives are back in order now and you're first to make a declaration of independence. That's part of what you're trying to tell me, isn't it? That you were certainly never in love with me?"

She shook her head, hurt choking her. Pride wrapped around her like a cold gray fog. To admit to love now, when he was all but saying she'd never been more than a temporary need for him? "And you certainly never loved me, did you, Mike? Since we're being so honest? I mean, it would have been pretty foolish to fall in love with each other, when we're so completely different, coming from completely different worlds—"

"Love's always a dangerous illusion."

"Yes." He certainly didn't have to tell her that.

"Honesty's better," Mike snapped. "It's the only thing you can count on when the whole damn rest of the world falls apart."

"Yes!" She bit off the word like a snake.

He didn't hear, because he was already gone. She heard the sound of his footsteps on the stairs at the same moment tears filled her eyes. Ships that passed in the night? Oh, Ianelli, that's really all I ever was to you?

Ten

Another set of car doors slammed, sending Maggie flying for the steps. After two days of rain, the puddles were like mirrors and the grass glistened under a lazy August sun; soft clouds skimmed a pure aquamarine sky. The weather went unappreciated and unnoticed. Every time she'd heard a car door slam since noon, she'd panicked it would be Mike, arriving before she was ready for him.

It wasn't Mike. Four people climbed out of the car, three men and a woman. Maggie fixed a smile as she approached them. A perfectly terrible idea seemed to be going increasingly downhill.

The three men were clearly Ianellis, but they were so totally unlike Mike that her heart sank yet again. The oldest was wearing a sport coat loud enough to wake the dead. Another was tippling from a silver flask—his party had obviously already started. And the third, the youngest man, was standing legs apart, hands on hips, as though daring the world to be exciting enough for him.

Wearing white sharkskin with diamonds in her ears, the blond woman was tall and tanned. Her face creased in a smile when she spotted Maggie. "You have to be Margaret Mary Flannery?"

"That's Maggie—and yes, I'm the lady who invited all of you. I'm so glad you could come."

"Most fun thing we've all done in ages. And when you wrote us that letter all about Joseph's whorehouse and treasure hunting and gambling and gangsters . . . well." Her laugh was light and breezy. "The Ianelli clan has traveled more miles than this for a party. Family reunions are just too rare to miss. But never mind that, I should be introducing us. I'm Julia; Gordon's my husband—and if you're trying to keep the family tree straight, Gordon's one of Joseph Ianelli's sons and Mike's uncle. Rafe is Mike's brother, Tony's his cousin. . . ."

Maggie shook hands and smiled, but the names went right over her head. Who cared? More than thirty people had descended on her since noon. Names were the least of her worries. "Come in," she encouraged the four. "I've set up picnic tables by the river; there are drinks in the house—"

"Your family's here, too?" Julia questioned.

"Yes, that was the idea. That both Flannerys and Ianellis might enjoy seeing the place that was once a part of both families. In a few more weeks, it wouldn't be possible . . . as I think I mentioned in the letter, I'll be running a business out of here." Maggie said wryly, "All of you are my trial run. I hoped that if I could take on the sheer numbers of the two clans—"

"That you could handle anything?" Julia said with a laugh. "Believe me, it would take a braver soul than me to try it, if your Flannery clan is as large as ours."

"Well, obviously everyone couldn't manage the distance. . . ." Maggie pushed open the door, ushering everyone in. The noise level inside the house spoke for how many *had* taken her up on her invitation.

She took one last frantic glance at the drive. Mike wasn't due to get out of work for at least another hour. If and when he did arrive, he wasn't expecting a family reunion but a plumbing crisis.

There was no plumbing crisis. The ruse to get Mike here was a lie. Maggie had been living with Ianelli's particular brand of honesty for the last month and a half. Such honesty, she'd discovered, was the pits. So was holding on to pride, self respect, integrity and the ridiculous idea of living without him.

Finding a way to get a strong, scrupulously honest man of integrity to believe in her brand of fantasies was a slight problem. A few weeks ago she'd conceived of a family reunion. His family had to matter to him and she could show him how well she got on with them. She could subtly remind him that the Ianellis and Flannerys had been successfully allied in another generation, and that whole illusion of to-getherness would...oh, hell.

It was a terrible idea. She'd been desperate. It was possible she'd had worse ideas in her life than this party, but until the families had started arriving, she'd had no idea how bad a bad idea could be.

"Maggie?"

With a brilliant smile, Maggie rushed inside to join her guests. On the surface, the gathering was going beautifully. Party lovers recognized party lovers. People impulsive enough to travel hundreds of miles for an impromptu weekend in a retired house of ill re-pute already had something in common. Italian bru-nettes bussed Irish redheads in an instant spirit of camaraderie and the noise level was deafening.

She made an attempt at introductions for the sake of the new arrivals. "This is my mother, Barbara... my brother Blake and his wife, Laura...Andrea is my sister...." Her soft voice didn't begin to dent the cacophony of other voices and abruptly she gave up.

She righted a lamp on her way to the kitchen. There, unpacking a carton of liquor bottles, was Ned. He just looked at her accusingly.

"Look, they'll calm down after they've been here awhile," she said firmly.

"You know how much liquor they been through before it was even high noon?"

"They're just having fun."

"Two of them are out in the river without a stitch of clothes on."

Maggie touched her temples. "Yes, well...it's hot." Grabbing a tray of canapes, she pushed through the door into the dining room ahead, and tried not to wince at the noise.

Barbara tugged her daughter's arm. "What a manager you are, darling! I can't imagine how you accomplished all of this!" She murmured, "That cousin of your Michael's is just a bit of a drinker, I'm afraid. And I understand the one boy was actually in jail for passing a bad check. Imagine—"

Maggie dragged a hand through her hair. "He's not 'my' Michael, Mom."

She just hadn't realized how fast the whole thing would get out of hand. Mike's relatives weren't bad. It was her family that was causing the problems. Blake could charm a snake, but he was outdrinking everyone in sight. Her sister Andrea was an incredible beauty, but color flooded Maggie's face as she watched Andrea thrust amazingly perfect cleavage in the face of the Ianelli whose lap she was sitting on. Laura, Blake's wife, was one of those skinny-dipping in the river, heaven knew with whom.

And her house, her beautiful house.... At seven o'clock that morning, the house had looked perfect. Downstairs, brass and crystal chandeliers gleamed; long velvet draperies had been elegantly pulled back with tassels; fringed carpets adorned the polished hardwood floors. The four rooms she intended to use as conference rooms were all open, revealing the many decorating touches she'd used to maintain the '30s feeling. One casino table had been cut down to make a desk; the other had been converted into a wet bar in the dining room. A collage of '30s gangsters and their molls decorated the stairs; the boa scarf had been framed and hung; the old trunks had been restrapped and polished and were used as end tables.

Now, people were sitting everywhere from the mantel to the floor. At least three drinks had already spilled; a tray of food had tipped over. The dried flower arrangement she'd set in an empty bottle of 1923 Rothschild was being used as an ashtray.

She heard a crash from upstairs and looked up with alarm. The only room she'd had the sense to lock up was the madam's room.

"Maggie, this is terrific," Andrea hissed in her ear. "Who'd have guessed the family sweetheart could put on such a bash? Good for you, darling!"

"I'm glad you're having a good time." Maggie took another worried look out the window, then glanced back with a tense smile. "Andrea, if I could just get the group outside, I think . . ."

He was there, suddenly, standing in the doorway. He was still wearing a dark business suit and the tired lines looked white around his eyes. He looked strong, shrewd, good-looking, sexy, indomitable. And mad as hell. Mike's eyes caught hers, and Maggie shrank inside.

"Who," Andrea whispered, "is *that*? Never mind, darling. I'll find out all on my own."

For the next three hours, Mike saw Maggie carrying trays of food outside, refilling bottles for the bar, and dealing poker hands. She was wearing a sun dress, and that flash of spring green, along with a whirl of dark copper hair and a sparkle of green eyes, showed up everywhere. She managed to be any place he wasn't, and she managed to move very fast.

He saw her listen to Gordon chortling stories about cheating the IRS, and he saw her nodding patiently while Rafe explained how to work a good swindle in the used-car business. He saw her duck Tony's alcoholic pass.

Her kin weren't so bad. They were a little loud and her sister had a small problem keeping her hands to herself, but overall they were a lively group who obviously simply loved a party.

Mike didn't... not this kind of party. He'd anticipated a quiet two-hour talk with Maggie. He'd expected a plumbing crisis, but he hadn't really cared why she'd asked him here. The only thing that mattered was that she *had* asked him. Hope, he hadn't known existed had soared like a 747 during his ride here. Need seemed a key. For the last month and a half, he'd desperately hoped that she'd see she needed more than a lover.

It didn't take him five minutes to see she needed him for nothing. Dinner for some thirty people didn't faze her; controlling the rowdiest Ianellis didn't make her blink; three hours of wall-to-wall noise didn't bother her. He'd caught her looking at him once, during an awkward moment when her sister had chosen to drape herself somewhere near his body for reasons he couldn't fathom. Maggie had looked, smiled, disappeared.

Around nine, his headache won. His relatives had played the reunion thing for all it was worth, and he'd had it with noise and smoke. He headed outside.

The sky was jet black and the light of the stars was too faint to brighten the path so he waited until his eyes adjusted. For a few minutes he simply breathed in fresh air. The river was wafting in a cold breeze; it always chilled at night this close to the river, even in August. He started walking.

The grass had no dew yet, and so it still felt warm and springy from its afternoon soak in the sun. After several days of rain, the textures outside were invariably soft. The grass, the leaves, the way bushes rubbed together in the summer wind made little sound, all more whisper than rustle. Brooding silence poured over him, through him.

The dogwood was no longer in flower, but there was a familiar hickory next to it, and its trunk made the best of backrests. He leaned back with a sigh, and had almost closed his eyes when the shadow beneath the opposite tree shifted nervously. The sprite he'd been trying to catch up with all evening didn't do a very good job at fading into the bark.

"I wouldn't," he suggested slowly, "try to run."

Maggie wrapped her arms around her legs. The worst part about being discovered was knowing she'd desperately wanted to be discovered. "I wasn't going to run." She said helplessly, "Oh, Mike, I thought it would be such a nice surprise, and instead it was absolutely the wrong thing to do, wasn't it?"

"Honey, what were you trying to do? Why on earth didn't you tell me you were inviting all of them? For that matter—why did you?"

"For lots of reasons." She was too discouraged and tired to make up clever answers. "Your family have a reunion every year, so do mine—this seemed a great place to have it, where they could all enjoy sharing what our grandfathers were up to."

He paused and then said, "And there were other reasons?"

"Yes." She plucked a handful of grass, let it sift through her fingers, and groped helplessly for the right words. "I kept thinking about our grandfathers. About how being two very different people didn't stop our grandfathers from getting along, from creating something special. They built on a fantasy, Mike, a fantasy where you could believe in magic while you were here. But it was never real magic. It was a Flannery and an Ianelli who made their own private world." Then she added swiftly, "And you're never going to convince me that what they did was immoral or wrong..."

"I wouldn't try," he said softly. Offhand, he couldn't think of anything he wanted to change about Maggie. He just wanted her close—where they could discuss all her fantasies. Until she'd started talking to him, he'd had no idea how fast hopelessness could disappear.

"And I thought, if I brought the families together again, you'd see that Flannery and Ianelli magic. I thought—your family must be important to you. I thought—you'd see that we all got along. I—"

"Maggie, I don't give a hoot in hell if you get along with my family and never did. They're a bunch of derelicts. Now would you kindly come over here?"

She shook her head. "Nope."

"This is a better tree trunk to lean against."

"This one's just fine."

"There's a better view of the moon from this tree."

"There isn't any moon to—"

"I love you, Maggie."

The breeze picked up the sound of his words. Leaves stirred. The grass took on those first diamonds of night dew, and Maggie was staring at those dew drops when two large feet wandered in front of her vision. Silently Mike crouched down. His eyes were as black as the night, but the night had never had that tender shine. His fingers sifted through the dark copper strands of her hair. "I more than love you, little one," he said softly. "I adore you. And I never needed any gathering of the Ianellis and the Flannerys to remind me that those names belong together as a matched set."

She raised her eyes, curling her cheek to the shape of his palm. Softness filled her throat. She couldn't talk. He'd take it back if she tried to talk.

"Maggie, I thought that's what you were doing—all you were doing . . . believing in magic. I loved being your lover, but I couldn't be just a fantasy, little one. I'm flesh and blood. I make too many mistakes; I come with a scar on my name. And I was afraid you weren't facing that honestly..."

"Oh, Mike." She shook her head fiercely, tears spraying on his hand. "I fell in love with you that first day, the flesh and blood man. You're the first and only man I ever met who ever just let me be me. Maggie. The Maggie I want to be and can be and just am. And when you didn't contact me after I went back to Philadelphia, I nearly died."

"I couldn't. I told you. I not only didn't have a job, but I had a label of thief around my neck. I had nothing to offer you, little one, and besides, I didn't believe you wanted the man, but a lover. You knew nothing about me, Maggie. I thought you were caught up in fantasies about a lover...."

He lowered her to the grass. She didn't resist. He leaned over her, locking her in with his arms. He liked the look of her hair against the cool velvet green. He liked the smell of earth and wind and river close to Maggie. All of it was real. None of it was more vulnerable than the green crystals in her eyes.

"I knew everything about you," she said fiercely. "Everything that mattered to me. But..." She reached up to trace his stubborn jaw with her finger. He needed a shave. At night after work he always needed a shave. And he needed sleep; there were circles under his eyes. The man looked like he hadn't slept in weeks. He was so...dear. "I was ashamed," she whispered. "For throwing myself at you. I didn't believe you could care back, Mike. Not about me."

"About the woman who stuffed her sweater with toilet paper? About the woman who carried a grocery store in a duffel bag and yelled at a total stranger for taking on the world alone?" His lips came closer, close enough that his breath hovered over hers, sweet and familiar. "You thought I didn't care, Maggie? I adored you. You were so damned real. You turned my world right side up again." He hesitated. A wicked, lazy grin gradually formed on his lips. "Although you did rather throw yourself at me, didn't you? In fact, I think I'm going to tell our children what a brazen hussy you were. And our grandchildren. And our great—"

"Mike." She touched her fingers to his lips to stop the kiss. She had to be absolutely sure he understood. "That was just for you. You were the man I wanted to make love to. Not a fantasy.... And not just any man. You."

He absorbed that, looking into her eyes. "So it was a man you wanted to make love to, was it?"

"Yes."

"A man who makes mistakes, Maggie. A man who other people have branded a thief. If you think you're getting a saint—"

"Ianelli, my whole childhood was filled with saints. Holy St. Patrick, are you going to hover there all night or are you going to kiss me?"

He kissed her. Ianelli did know how to kiss. His lips skimmed along her temple, her cheek, then closed on her mouth. His arms wrapped her up, so tight. She could smell the river and Mike, and the grass and

Mike. The world turned fragile. Mike was infinitely solid. Forbidden fantasies were sweet, but never as sweet as reality. He kissed like love and there was just no room for doubt, not anymore.

"Little one?"

"Hmmmm?"

"I'm seriously afraid I smell smoke."

"So do I," she murmured and locked closer.

"Maggie?"

"They're going home tomorrow," she promised him.

"Maggie."

"Damnation."

He laughed, pulling away from her. Once he was standing, he pulled her to her feet. The house in the far distance was all lit up, and echoed sounds traveled to where they were. Wood smoke fluttered in the still air, faint but unmistakable. She looked at Mike, her smile dying, and then they were off.

A quiet walk became quick steps, then a dead run. The screen door to the veranda banged behind both of them when they raced inside. The smoke was heavier inside, and the entire gathering of the clans had clustered in the far room by the river.

"Maggie! Michael! We've been looking all over for you!" Barbara shook her head wildly. "It became so cool—Gordon thought he'd start a little fire in the fireplace. There was wood out on the porch—"

They'd never tried that one fireplace. Mike, who'd surged through the crowd ahead of her, was already kneeling down, spreading the few smoking sticks in the hearth. He glanced up and around until he spotted her suddenly white face and winked. No crisis here, his eyes promised her.

She relaxed. A pan of water and the last of the small fire was out. The smoke smell still hovered in the room, but the river breeze was fast sending the scent out the open windows. Subdued conversations gradually started again, but Maggie inched forward, unsure why Mike was still fussing at the hearth.

"The damper's sticking," he told her when she finally reached his side. "It stuck last winter; I forgot all about it. It's like there's something in there, preventing it from closing."

"Bats?" she whispered.

"Not bats, you goose." He bent down and reached his arm up into the chimney.

"Goose? How dare you call me a goose, Ianelli—and what on earth are you doing?"

"Bricks are loose. That seems to be what the problem was all along. This fireplace wasn't safe to begin with."

Her face paled with images of the serious fire that could have been. They paled even more when his soot-darkened hand brought something down from the inside of the chimney. At first glance, it looked like a tarnished brass brick. At second glance, it looked more gold than brass.

For the first time in hours, there were at least three seconds of total silence in the house. Thirty people tried to push and pull in an effort to see the heavy bar of gold bullion in Mike's hands. Maggie was only interested in looking at his eyes. "Gramps's treasure?" she whispered.

The silence couldn't last. A low murmur became an excited buzz, then turned to laughter as someone popped a lid off a champagne bottle and the group descended. Mike laid down the bar, whispered something to her mother, and ducked through the crowd to reach Maggie's side. "We're leaving," he told her.

"Now?"

"Now."

He pushed her toward the back door, back out into the night and toward the river. Bewildered, she couldn't figure out where he intended to go until her right foot all but collided with the first outside stair.

At the top of the iron steps, she perched her fanny on the windowsill and swung her legs inside. Mike was beside her almost before she'd caught her breath. Before she'd started breathing he'd already pushed down the straps to her sundress, was searching her back for the zipper. "The door's locked?" he demanded.

She nodded. "I couldn't let anyone else in here."

Her dress whooshed to the floor. Below, she could hear the muted but unmistakably jubilant sounds of celebration. Here there was just silence and the flicker of blue silk draperies at the windows. The lonely madam's room that waited far too long for lovers. Maggie shivered all over, her fingers fumbling at his shirt buttons.

"He didn't lie to me," she whispered.

"Your grandfather?"

She nodded, and felt his lips on her neck, a slow and savoring kiss that did absolutely nothing to stop the shivers from chasing through her.

"I don't think," Mike murmured, "that either of our grandfathers gave a damn about gold bullion."

"No?"

She was cold, standing there. He swept her up and dropped her with gentle determination on the mattress, then moved back to take off the rest of his clothes. Before he joined her, he tugged the tassles around the bed. It was past time to enclose the two of them in blue silk, and dark as it was, he could see Maggie's sudden smile.

It was a wicked smile. A smile that boded ill for his future as a sane man, a smile that challenged him as a lover, and that promised him more love than he'd ever envisioned in a lifetime. He dropped down beside her, for a moment not touching.

"Our grandfathers," he said lazily, "were brilliant men."

"You think so?"

He nodded. "I think they both knew what they were doing, sweet. Some treasures really aren't all that valuable. Some treasures you simply have to turn back to the government. That's no fun—"

She drew in her breath. "No?"

"Some treasures," Mike said softly, "you get to keep for a lifetime. Let's hear it, Maggie."

"I love you," she whispered.

"That's what I was waiting for." He murmured, "Are you going to be a very bad woman for me, little one?"

"Very bad," she affirmed. "How could I be anything else in this room? Any woman who sleeps in here has to be wicked. Amoral. Brazen."

"For a lifetime?"

"For a lifetime."

"Because I'm never letting you go, you know. We're going to make babies in this bed."

"That's the first I've heard about that," she mentioned interestedly. "Lots of them?"

"Lots of them."

"You're going to be very tired, Ianelli," Maggie said demurely. "Perhaps you'd better rest up. Starting now."

He chuckled, and wrapped himself up in endless green eyes and a good woman. She had no idea how happy he intended to make her. None.

**Available
January 1987**

NEVADA
SILVER

The third book in the exciting
Desire Trilogy by Joan Hohl.

The Sharp brothers are back, along with
sister Kit...and Logan McKittrick.

Kit's loved Logan all her life and, with a little
help from the silver glow of a Nevada night,
she must convince the stubborn rancher that
she's a woman who needs a man's love—not
the protection of another brother.

Don't miss *Nevada Silver*—Kit and
Logan's story and the conclusion
of Joan Hohl's acclaimed
Desire Trilogy.

DT-C-1